"And Why Aren't You Married?"

Charity asked brightly.

"Me?" Ross was taken aback. He thought for a moment and tried to recall some special lady, someone he might almost have married. He'd never realized before that there was no one. "I've been too busy," he muttered evasively.

"Doing what?" she prompted.

Ross stared at her. His gaze flickered over her trusting face, the soft hair that fell about her shoulders, the clinging nightgown that outlined her breasts. "All the wrong things, obviously."

Suddenly Ross realized that there was more to this masquerade than he'd expected. He lifted the wineglass he held, meeting hers in a toast. "Here's to our make-believe marriage," he said softly. "May it be short . . . but sweet."

Dear Reader:

Welcome! You hold in your hand a Silhouette Desire—your ticket to a whole new world of reading pleasure.

A Silhouette Desire is a sensuous, contemporary romance about passions, problems and the ultimate power of love. It is about today's woman—intelligent, successful, giving—but it is also the story of a romance between two people who are strong enough to follow their own individual paths, yet strong enough to compromise, as well.

These books are written by, for and about every woman that you are—wife, mother, sister, lover, daughter, career woman. A Silhouette Desire heroine must face the same challenges, achieve the same successes, in her story as you do in your own life.

The Silhouette reader is not afraid to enjoy herself. She knows when to take things seriously and when to indulge in a fantasy world. With six books a month, Silhouette Desire strives to meet her many moods, but each book is always a compelling love story.

Make a commitment to romance—go wild with Silhouette Desire!

Best,

Isabel Swift
Senior Editor & Editorial Coordinator

RAYE MORGAN
Husband for Hire

Silhouette Desire

Published by Silhouette Books New York

America's Publisher of Contemporary Romance

SILHOUETTE BOOKS
300 East 42nd St., New York, N.Y. 10017

ISBN: 0-373-05434-3

First Silhouette Books printing July 1988

Books by Raye Morgan

Silhouette Romance

Roses Never Fade #427

Silhouette Desire

Embers of the Sun #52
Summer Wind #101
Crystal Blue Horizon #141
A Lucky Streak #393
Husband for Hire #434

RAYE MORGAN

favors settings in the West, which is where she has spent most of her life. She admits to a penchant for western heroes, believing that whether he's a rugged outdoorsman or a smooth city sophisticate he tends to have a streak of wildness that the romantic heroine can't resist taming. She's been married to one of those western men for twenty years and is busy raising four more in her Southern California home.

One

"I...I need a man."

Ross Carpenter's eyebrows rose. The woman on the other end of the telephone line sounded strangely furtive. But considering her request, perhaps that was to be expected. He felt a moment's exasperation for having answered the call. He'd come into his sister Marlena's modern, colorfully decorated office only minutes before. She was out. Her secretary had gone to lunch. So he'd thrown himself down behind the desk to wait. And when the telephone had chimed, he'd answered automatically.

"Could you speak a little louder?" he asked, leaning back in the swivel chair and propping his soft Italian-leather shoes up on the desk. "I'm not sure I understand what you want."

"This *is* the Mayfair Temporary Employment Agency, isn't it?" Her voice was stronger now, as though by stating her needs so boldly she'd gotten over the worst part.

Ross glanced at the letterhead on the stationery of Marlena's company piled up alongside the computer keyboard, just checking. "Yes, you've reached the right number."

The woman on the line sighed. "This is so embarrassing. You probably think I'm crazy. But I really do need a man for a very special job. Do you have any available?"

Ross hesitated. The long, slender fingers of one hand curled around the receiver while those of the other combed through his thick, jet-black hair. It was on the tip of his tongue to tell her that he didn't think Mayfair was in the business of hiring out men for lonely women, but something in her voice stopped him.

Low and husky, it had an oddly appealing quality—and a lilt of humor. She sounded like a woman who knew how to laugh at herself. Perhaps this was really a joke. If so, he might as well string along for the punch line.

"What type of man did you have in mind?" he asked instead of putting her off.

"Good question." She laughed shortly. "I wish I knew. I've never had much luck judging men." She thought for a few seconds. "He should be tall, I guess, since I'm not exactly the china-doll type. Good looks would be nice." She laughed, and then her voice softened as she went on. "But you know what? I think intelligence is more important. Yes, definitely, intelligent eyes. That's what I want. Do you have anyone like that?"

"Perhaps." Ross gazed, bemused, into the mirror on the other side of the office. His own sea-blue eyes were filled with amusement, and a reluctant grin played on his wide mouth. He stopped that quickly enough, frowning instead. Why was he leading her on this way? The woman was an obvious head case. He should refer her to the psycho ward at Cottage Hospital. He hesitated, but for some reason he went on with the charade instead. "About what age are you looking for?"

"Well, I'm thirty-two. What do you think? Anything over that up to about forty. Or anything, really, that seems compatible." She sounded so damn reasonable. "I've never hired a husband before." She sighed. "I know this isn't your usual request. I did think of calling an escort service, but that seemed so sleazy." She cleared her throat, steadying herself. "Okay, I'll try to list the essential qualities." She paused, then went on. "Good-looking, charming, good manners. That about covers it. Oh, and he's got to look successful. You know what I mean? Someone an older woman would put a lot of faith in."

Reasonable but confusing. Ross's forehead furled with puzzlement. "An older woman?"

"Yes, you see, my Aunt Doris..." She sighed again. "But you don't want to hear about that. Suffice it to say I need someone who's obvious husband material. I'll pay the going rate. How soon can you send him over?"

This was obviously no joke. The woman was serious. Ross sighed, glancing at the clock on the wall. An appealing voice could take him only so far. He had other things to do with his life, and it was time to cut this short. "You know," he said smoothly, "it's really a shame, but we've had a run on our male temps lately. I'm afraid we're fresh out."

"Really?" Her disappointment almost made him feel sorry for her. "You don't have anyone at all?"

"No one at all."

"Not even a younger man...?"

"No. And not even an older man."

She sighed. "Can you take my name and number and call me if you have a cancellation?"

There was no point to it. Cancellations on make-believe husbands were few and far between. But still, Ross hesitated, then grabbed a pen up off the blotter. "Sure," he said shortly, ready to be rid of her but not ready to employ the quelling rudeness he might have used with someone else. "Your name?"

"If someone was available even just part-time—"

"Your name?" he repeated impatiently.

"Ames."

He wrote the letters down in a careless scrawl, then stared at them. Something was ringing a bell in the back of his memory. "Ames. A-M-E-S?" he asked, still staring.

"Yes."

He frowned. "First name?"

"Charity." His eyes widened. His fingers gripped the receiver more tightly as he jotted the name down. "And what is your occupation, Miss Ames?" he asked evenly, his gaze fixed, every muscle tense.

She seemed to be startled by the question. "What do you need that for?"

He shifted the receiver from one ear to the other. "Rules, Miss Ames. Forms must be filled out."

"Oh," she said doubtfully. "Well, there's no harm in telling you, I suppose. I run a restaurant. The Golden Tiger on Dos Pueblos Port Pier."

Ross leaned back in the chair. His face relaxed and very slowly his lips formed the silent word. *Bingo!*

"Hello?"

"Yes," he said hurriedly, straightening again. "Just a moment, Miss Ames." His mind worked furiously, one idea after another flying through. What an incredible coincidence. He ought to pinch himself, see if he were actually dreaming. What an opportunity! Now if only he could grasp it.... "It seems you are in luck. I've just realized one of our best men is available after all."

"Oh, wonderful." If Ross had been a compassionate man, he would have felt a twinge of guilt for the relief in her voice. "How soon can you get him over here?"

Ross glanced back at the clock. "Three this afternoon."

"Perfect. Aunt Doris isn't actually arriving for several days, but I want to get our stories straight and get things set up before she gets here." Her voice now brimmed with excitement. "What's his name?"

"His name?" Ross thought fast. He'd never actually had any face-to-face dealings with the lady, but others had on his behalf. She might recognize the name. "Ross...Ross Parker." He supplied himself with his mother's maiden name.

"Great name." She sounded eager to get to work. "What does he look like?"

"Oh..." Ross stared into the mirror again, suddenly feeling an uncharacteristic flicker of embarrassment. "Average, I guess," he said gruffly. "Six-four. Dark hair. Blue eyes. Intelligent eyes," he added quickly.

Charity Ames was nothing if not enthusiastic. "I love him already!"

He blinked. "What exactly did you have in mind?" he asked suspiciously.

"I told you. I need a husband for about four or five days. That's all. He'll have to stay here with me, of course, to make it look good. And when Aunt Doris goes back to New York—"

"A quickie divorce."

She laughed. "Something like that."

Ross nodded in satisfaction. The setup was perfect. A couple of days to soften her up, a few more to convince her. "Let me have your address," he said quickly. "And we'll send your hired husband right over."

He stared at the telephone for a long moment after they'd hung up. It couldn't be this easy. After all those months of trying to pin Charity Ames down, of trying to get a private meeting to present his offer, of getting the brush-off at every turn, he'd suddenly been given a free ticket right into her living room. There had to be a catch.

"Hello, darling." Marlena, his lovely, black-haired sister, breezed into the office. A cloud of sultry perfume seemed to settle about her as she came to a halt and leaned down to kiss her musing brother. Not a hair was out of place. Her makeup was pearly and exact. The suit hugging her slender body was cut to fit only her. She moved with the confidence of a woman who had gone to the best schools, had been the belle of her debutante ball and had name recognition at all the most expensive shops in town.

"I hope you haven't been waiting for too long," she told her brother. "I had to check with the printers on some ads we're running."

Ross looked up with narrowed eyes. "What do you think of when I mention Charity Ames of the Golden Tiger?" he asked softly.

Marlena shrugged. "Isn't that the one holdout from implementing your grand plan for the Dos Pueblos Port Pier development?" she asked. "I know all the other restaurants and shops out there joined your Commercial Growth Organization, and you were so furious that the Ames woman wouldn't even consider your offers."

"Exactly."

Marlena sank onto the corner of her desk, her pretty face puckered with worry. "Oh, Ross, what does it matter if one restaurant holds out? Just ignore the crazy woman. Remember how everything turned out with the Ojai project? It's a masterpiece. All the business and architectural magazines have written it up. Dos Pueblos will be the same. Once your plan gets rolling, she'll be begging to be involved."

"Maybe," he said slowly, but he wasn't really listening. He was thinking over his list of options as though he were flipping through the cards in a Rolodex. He knew he could go forward with the Dos Pueblos project without Charity Ames, but he was a man who didn't like to lose. The Golden Tiger would always be a flaw in his scheme if she didn't come around. He wanted her in, and he was ready to do what he had to do to make sure she joined.

For a moment Marlena watched the process she knew so well, and then she leaned forward and waved a hand in front of his face. "Hello, anyone home?" she called.

He looked up in surprise. "What?"

"Remember me? I thought I was the one you came to see."

His frown told her he didn't appreciate having his thoughts interrupted, which was just what she'd expected. Slipping off the desk, she took the face of her younger brother between her two hands and smiled sadly down into it.

"When was the last time you spent an entire day without thinking about business?" she asked. "Ross Carpenter, you're almost forty and you might as well be eighty-two. You never have any fun. You never do anything silly just for the hell of it. You take life much too seriously, darling, and you're not even listening to me now, are you?"

Ross stared at her blankly, his mind miles away.

Her laugh was rueful as she rumpled his hair. "Oh, well, come on, let's go to lunch. I can talk. You can ignore me. We'll have a marvelous time."

Ross seemed to see her at last. "Oh. Sorry, Marlena. I can't have lunch today. I don't have time." He rose, patted her absently and started for the door. "Charity Ames has asked me to be her husband," he called back, shrugging, his face still furrowed in thought. "And I guess I'm going to do it. I'm on my way over there now."

Marlena made a strangled, gurgling sound, but no real words came out. He left the office, whistling as he went down the hall to the elevator. He'd never been a husband before and he wasn't sure just what it entailed, but he was ready to try. The Ames holdout had been a thorn in his side for too long. He had a growing conviction that if he played this one just right, he was about to pluck it out.

"Well, I don't know." Mason shook his elegantly shaggy head of hair doubtfully as he gazed about the room from his vantage point on the long sectional couch. Sunlight was streaming in through the high windows, but there was still an air of gloom and doom to the place. "Maybe if you took a blowtorch to your entire apartment you could convince Aunt Doris you'd had a fire and were now in the midst of repairs. I don't see any other hope for it."

Charity Ames threw herself down on the other end of the couch and glared at her brother. "Don't make fun of my decorating," she said. "It looked great when I first did it."

Mason laughed and rolled off the couch to sit cross-legged on the floor. "I don't mean to be snide, Char, but that must have been a long, long time ago."

Charity looked around the room at the elongated paintings and the tall, contorted sculpture of a strange human form in the corner. The couch was low and formless, and huge pillows served as chairs on the other side of the slab of slate that formed her coffee table.

"I was in the middle of my blue period then," she said with dreamy remembrance. "I was searching for meaning, searching for goals. That's why everything's done up in long lines and indigo." She sighed. "Looks kind of bleak now, doesn't it?"

"Kind of," he said with emphasis. "Am I to take it that you're over that lost, melancholy stuff?"

"Oh, yes." Charity smiled at her sibling, and when she smiled, her dark eyes could light up a room. "I've got the restaurant now. It's filled my life. And I know what I want now, where I'm going." She laughed softly. "I guess you could call this my in-the-pink phase."

Mason groaned, closing his eyes and grimacing. "Just don't let it show in any new color schemes you might be contemplating," he advised. "Happiness is one thing. Frothy pink walls is another."

"No pink," she promised. "But what exactly am I going to do? I don't really have time for an overhaul before Aunt Doris gets here."

Mason shrugged, leaning against the couch. He had an inborn facility for relaxing that reminded Charity of a cat. Mason could fall asleep anywhere, and if she didn't watch out, he'd do it now.

"Come on," she urged, nudging him with her foot. "After all, you're the one who got me into this predicament."

He raised both hands in the air, palms open. *"Mea culpa,"* he acknowledged. "I did make up that story about you being happily married. But I never dreamed the dear old girl would make a run out here to see for herself."

"Neither did I, or I would have told her the truth from the start." Charity sighed. "But once you'd told her, it seemed so harmless to just let the story stick...."

"You should have contradicted me right away," Mason said with innocent aplomb that made Charity want to hit him with a pillow. "Everybody knows what a flake I am. She wouldn't have thought twice." His grin was wicked. "But once *you'd* acquiesced, the tale might as well have been written in stone."

Charity kicked him a little harder. "I don't know what you thought you could gain by such a ridiculous story, anyway," she grumbled.

"I didn't do it for me. It was for her."

"Oh, really?" Charity picked up her glass of iced tea and took a long sip, her dark eyes examining her brother's face. He'd always been good-looking, but now there was something else in his face that disturbed her—a look of weary bitterness around the eyes, a line of sadness around the mouth. Mason was a dilettante, a playboy, a drifter. And that was all he would ever be. She ought to accept that and stop caring, but she couldn't. She loved him. "Convince me."

He shrugged his shoulders. "You know what she's like. She can't believe we all turned out the way we did."

Charity's laugh was short and had a bitter edge. She couldn't believe it, either, even though she'd seen the direction from the beginning. "I don't know why it should be a big surprise to her. After all, with parents like we had—"

"That's just it." He smiled ruefully at his sister. They had always been close and they had a shorthand way of talking to each other that could shut out others if they didn't watch it. A wink, an elbow jab, could speak volumes and make words almost unnecessary. "She wants us to be different. I think she's always had some personal fantasy about being the dominant force in our lives, the one who was going to change us back into normal people—"

"Hah!"

"And then she looks us over. There's Faith with her ideas of living on herbs out in the desert, and there's me with my nomadic life-style and what she would consider a frivolous career...."

Charity set down her glass with a snap. "And there's me running a restaurant and being a good, solid citizen. Why couldn't you leave it at that?"

"Because she seemed to need more." Mason straightened and turned so that Charity could see the earnest expression on his face. "Listen, we were there in her apartment in Boston, sitting around the dinner table, and she'd invited all her friends over to meet me. They'd turned up their noses at the ski bum—you know how people do— and every one of them had a daughter or a niece who was married to a heart surgeon. I...I just felt bad for Aunt Doris. It's not her fault we turned out so weird. So—"

"So you invented something for her to be proud of, too."

His grin was handsomely sheepish. "Yeah. I mean, what you're doing may seem normal and mainstream in the eighties, but that's not the decade Aunt Doris lives in. To her it's still 1955, and in 1955 good girls get married to men who'll protect them."

Charity groaned. "So you told her I was married."

"To a wonderful man."

"And now she's coming to meet him."

"Well..." Mason shrugged. "That's your problem. I'm getting out of town. You'll just have to explain that your husband is away at a business convention or something equally inane...."

"No, I won't." Charity enjoyed seeing her brother blink in surprise. It was so seldom that she succeeded in stopping him in his tracks. "I've found myself a husband. Aunt Doris will not be disappointed."

Mason was skeptical. "What, some friend who's offered to step in and play the part?"

"No." Charity made him wait a few seconds longer before filling him in. "Actually I've hired someone."

"What?"

"From a temporary agency."

"There are agencies where they rent out husbands?"

"Why not?" She enjoyed confounding him and didn't bother to explain it was actually an ordinary temporary agency.

Mason shook his head, a grin splitting his face. "Have you seen him?"

She hesitated. "No, but I'm sure he'll be perfectly presentable."

Mason groaned and fell back against the couch. "He'll be a gargoyle," he prophesied mournfully. "He'll have warts on his nose and wear a bowling shirt. Just what kind of man do you think would pursue a career hiring out as a temporary husband!"

Charity frowned. She hadn't considered that angle. "I . . . I'm sure he'll be just fine," she said uncertainly. What if Mason were right? What if she'd saddled herself with some monstrosity?

Mason hooted. "I'm sure he won't!"

Charity glared at him. "But as you said, it's my problem, isn't it? You won't even be here to help me get through the mess you created."

He grinned, shaking his head. "I wish I could stay and see this," he chortled. "It'll be the Three Stooges revisited. But Paul Lomax is coming by at around two, and we're heading for the airport."

She shook her head. "Yes, Chile is so lovely in winter," she said sharply. "Give my best to the dictator."

He turned palms up again, giving her the boyish, innocent smile that had captivated hearts all over the world. "Hey, can I help it if the best skiing is in South America this time of year? I gotta go where the action is."

"A man's gotta do what a man's gotta do." Charity's sarcasm was softened by the tousling she did to her brother's hair as she passed on her way to the kitchen. "And a woman's gotta stay behind to pick up the pieces."

He rose, actually helping her take dishes to the sink. "But you're so good at it," he said in what was supposed to be a soothing tone. "You always were the one to fix things for us."

He went on talking about the arrangements he and Paul had made for their trip to Chile, but Charity wasn't listening. His last words echoed in her mind. *You always were the one to fix things.* . . .

Twinges of rebellion stirred inside her. She swept a stack of dishes into the sudsy water and began to rub them vigorously with a dishcloth, but she couldn't clean away her thoughts as easily.

It was true. Though she was the youngest of three children, she'd always been the one with the level head, the one the others turned to as an anchor in the storm. Mason, being the male and two years older than Charity, should perhaps have been the natural leader of their little family, but it hadn't worked that way. Mason was a thrill seeker. He didn't believe in caution. More than once, Charity had been forced to pluck him from the jaws of sure disaster— or the local jail.

Their sister Faith was the oldest by another two years. Tradition said that the oldest should be the wisest and most responsible. Tradition had never dealt with Faith.

"She was left here by Martians on a field trip," Mason used to complain when they were teenagers. "No human species could have spawned this mutant aberration."

Faith was beautiful. Her blond hair floated around her in an unearthly cloud and her pale blue eyes seemed to see into another world, although they seldom saw what was going on around her.

They'd grown up on the run, moving from one Pacific island to another with parents who were, by turns, missionaries of a metaphysical religion, extortionists or con artists. There was no nice way of saying it. The Ameses had been crooks, and they'd raised their children in a weird atmosphere of cunning and chaos, usually just one step ahead of disaster—and the authorities.

Faith and Mason had never minded it much. Normal life seemed boring to them, anyway. Charity had felt the brunt of the burden; she'd ached for some dignity and respect. And so Charity had been the one to fix things when she could. When things went wrong, both her siblings still showed up on her doorstep, expecting her to shelter them from the cold, cruel world. And she'd never turned either one of them down.

Now she had Aunt Doris coming. Aunt Doris didn't want to be sheltered. Aunt Doris wanted to check on things. And Charity felt like a student on the eve of final exams.

"Going to dress up for your gargoyle?" Mason asked in all innocence just before he left the kitchen.

"Gargoyles are people, too," she reminded him, glaring all the while. Actually she *was* planning to dress up. It was only around family members that she looked like a hobo. Before the world, she liked to present a more professional image.

Mason shrugged. "I'm going out to pick up some supplies for the trip. If Paul gets here before I get back, entertain him. Okay?"

"Sure," she answered absently, but she hardly heard the door slam as he left. Gargoyles. Who needed them? She stared at the telephone. Maybe it would be best if she canceled the hired husband after all.

Two

Ross climbed the stairs to Charity Ames's second-story apartment, feeling very much as he often did when playing racquetball, at the point when he began to note his opponent tiring. The exhilaration of victory hadn't started to sink in, but it was definitely in the offing.

Miss Charity Ames needed a service. He was about to provide that service and have a chance to soften up his subject at the same time. The combination of his charm and her gratitude would surely do the trick. The addition of the Golden Tiger to the consortium he'd organized was as good as in the bag.

The apartment building was of quality construction, but it had the long, low, anonymous look of so many modern buildings. Ross took the stairs instead of the elevator, enjoying the exercise it gave his long, powerful legs. He was an hour early, but once he'd made up his mind, he'd wanted to get going with his plan. At the top of the stairs, he located apartment 20 and was just about to reach for the buzzer when the door flew open.

Ross stepped back to avoid the feminine body that came bounding out into the hallway. His first impression was of a mass of golden hair flying about and a pair of very dark eyes peering at him questioningly. In her hand was a measuring tape already extended and ready for action.

"Charity Ames?" he asked.

Without any hesitation the woman stuck out her hand and took Ross's for a vigorous shake. "Hi," she said brightly. "You must be Paul, Mason's friend." She waved him in. "Mason went out to get some last-minute supplies, but he'll be right back. Come on in. I'm just in the middle of taking some measurements of my living room."

Caught off guard, it took a moment for Ross to take in what she'd said. "No, actually..." he started, trying to correct her, let her know he wasn't this Paul person, but she wasn't listening. She'd already gone on to another subject.

"Could you hold this for me for a minute?" she asked, handing him the end of the tape measure. "Put it right here on the jamb. I'm trying to get accurate room dimensions." She watched as he did what she'd asked, nodded approvingly and began to pull out the tape, backing toward the far wall.

"Okay, let me stretch it out. I'm doing some fast remodeling—or at least I'm hoping to do some. As usual, I've waited until the last minute, so it's probably too late." She took her end of the tape measure to the windows at the opposite side of the apartment living room, measuring the width of the room. "Fourteen feet, six inches. Wouldn't you know it? Nothing is ever standard around here." She wrote down the figure in a notebook, and Ross watched, a bit bemused.

She wasn't quite what he'd expected. The dealings he'd had with her, though indirect, had made him picture her as cold, professional and extremely calculating—an icy, mature woman with absolutely no sex appeal. The Charity Ames on the telephone earlier that day had seemed a bit more scatterbrained, a little helpless, uncertain, and the two images hadn't gibed. Now he saw something completely different from either of those pictures.

The mop of hair was unruly, but she was hardly immature. The eyes, beneath straight, feathered brows, were coolly assessing, but a spark of humor revealed itself now and then. She was pretty, her features even, her expression alive. Her figure was slender, but full. She wore tight black slacks, a huge salmon-pink sweater, and her feet were bare.

"Listen," she said, glancing up at him again. One spray of her curly mop fell over her eye and she pushed it back with a quick shove. "Picture this..." She made a dramatic sweep with one hand. "A white shag rug. Really thick. You got it?" She glanced at him again, judging whether he was really paying attention. "Okay." She gestured in another direction. "A chrome-and-glass coffee table. With, unfortunately, this same old blue couch. What do you think?" Whirling, she confronted him, her dark eyes searching his. "How does that grab you?"

He was still standing in the open doorway of the apartment, and he hadn't quite got his bearings yet. Usually unflappable, he was unsteady here, and the factor that figured most strongly in that was the steady gaze from those brown eyes. "I don't know," he began doubtfully. She let out an explosive sigh, waving a hand as she marched across the room to look at it from another perspective.

"Okay, listen, the paintings will be off the wall. Gone. Instead..." She frowned, turning slowly to survey the entire room. "I'll put up framed posters of...oh, graphics of some sort. Colorful graphics. Rainbow colors and grinning faces. The sort of stuff you see all the time at your dentist's office." She looked up at him again. "What do you think?"

He hesitated, then shrugged. "Sounds fine to me."

She looked pained, shaking her head. "No good, huh? It just doesn't move you." She sank down onto the couch with a sigh, patting a place beside her in an invitation for him to sit.

She was casual. The invitation was offhand, friendly. And yet he felt a tiny twinge of excitement, something he hadn't felt in some time, though he'd been the recipient of many a much more sexy come-on. Suppressing the excitement, he sat.

"I know," she went on sadly, her attention all on her room. "I can't figure out what's happened! You know, I used to be so good at this kind of thing back when I was a poor, starving college student and all I had to contend with were bricks and boards." She laughed ruefully, remembering. "Now that I have enough money to do what I want, I've somehow lost the touch. And grown-up people aren't allowed to mess around with bricks and boards, are they?"

She smiled at him and he frowned. This wasn't the way it was supposed to go. He'd planned to come in and take charge of the situation, charming her, leading her in exactly the direction he needed her to go. Instead she'd thrown him off balance from the first, and he couldn't seem to regain his footing. He wasn't used to following along, and it annoyed him.

Her smile faded in the face of his frown, and she looked at him curiously, pulling her legs up under her on the couch and resorting to chattering as a way to smooth over the tension. He was beginning to make her nervous, and yet there was something compelling about the man. Not to mention sexy.

"What do you think?" she asked impulsively. "What style do you envision here? What sort do I look like to you?"

She held her chin out as though that would help him with her assessment. He found himself wanting to grin as he looked her over.

"South Sea Islands," he said suddenly. "I see you under palm fronds, in a sarong, with a flower in your hair."

The look of shock on her face surprised him. She stared at him for a long moment, wondering how he knew. Was it that obvious? But of course, she realized with a sense of relief. Mason must have told him about their background.

For the first time she began to look at her male visitor closely and to realize he wasn't at all what she would have expected in a friend of Mason's. This man seemed so...mature. He was wearing a suit, and a nice one at that. His eyes were as blue and as penetrating as lasers. Suddenly, she felt uncomfortable looking into them, and she dropped her gaze to his mouth. The lips were full, smooth, infinitely sensual. A wariness fluttered through her and she dropped her gaze again, this time to his strong, long-fingered hands, and for some silly reason her heart was pounding just a little too fast and she was breathless. Over Mason's friend? Heavens! What a thought.

Concentrating, she forced herself to calm down and went back to studying him. He didn't have the look of someone about to fly off to Chile for the skiing. A small, puzzled frown appeared between her brows. Mason was good-looking but insubstantial. Girls swooned, but women tended to narrow their eyes and read the basic instability beneath his charm. From what she'd heard about Paul, she'd expected much the same. And yet here he was, looking more like a high-powered business executive—even a business shark—than a ski bum.

"That's not me at all," she told him firmly. "I'm a professional woman." Her lip curled. "South Sea Islands is tacky!"

He shrugged. Something about Charity Ames was appealing to him mightily. Whether it was her warm, husky voice or her delicately hooked nose or her flashing dark eyes, he wasn't sure. He usually saw people in light of what they could do for him, how he could manipulate them. She wasn't playing fair. He wanted to reach out and shake her. And yet she made him smile.

"I can't help it," he told her frankly. "South Sea Islands is how I see you." He shrugged, wanting to explain so she wouldn't be offended. "Sort of fresh and breeze tossed..." This was a new role for him, and he was slightly embarrassed. "With a hint of the crispness of the sea...." His voice faded away and he grimaced, wishing he'd kept his mouth shut, but she smiled.

"You sound like a perfume commercial," she teased. She stared at him for a moment, appreciating his honesty. He was much older than she expected. There was something hard and resilient in him. She'd never been much of a leaner, but those broad shoulders looked as though they were made for leaning. Impulsive as always, she decided she could trust the man, despite the sensual appeal he was giving off. Sinking against the cushions again, she leaned toward him conspiratorially. "I'm sure Mason has also told you all about my problem...or, I should say, *our* problem. My darling brother is the one who instigated it."

Ross gazed at her blankly, not really sure just what she was talking about. "I'm not certain I know all about it," he said, feeling his way.

She gestured her disgust with the turn of affairs. "Well, it's come down to the point where I've had to consider *hiring* a husband. Can you believe that? I'm thinking of hiring a man to come and pretend to live with me for four or five days while Aunt Doris is here." She gazed at him, waiting for outrage, sympathy, anything that would make her feel a little better about what she was planning to do.

Ross stirred uncomfortably. It was definitely time to tell her who he was. "Charity," he began, "about the man you hired..."

Her eyes widened. "You already know about that? I hope Mason doesn't tell everyone in the building. Besides, I don't think I'm going through with it."

It was Ross's turn to be surprised. "You're not?"

She shook her head and her golden hair flew around like a net full of fireflies. "No. Mason predicts he'll look like a gargoyle, and when I thought about it, I had to agree. I mean, what kind of man would want to come do this sort of thing? Not anyone who had anything going in his life. What kind of man would want to give up five days to sit around and pretend to be married to me?"

"Oh, I don't know," he said gruffly, enjoying the look of her against his better judgment. "Just about any man who knew you, I'd think."

She waved a finger at him. "Now that's just it. That's what I thought of at first, picking a man I know. Except..." She frowned thoughtfully. "I don't know any who would do." She sighed, eyeing Ross speculatively. "The men I know are mostly business associates. I couldn't very well ask any of them to do this sort of thing."

"There must be someone," Ross said, trying to think of a way to turn the conversation to where he could tell her why he was here.

There's you, Charity thought. Once the idea had entered her mind, she felt a small stirring of excitement. Yes, this man would be perfect. He was tall, good-looking, confident—but he was also on his way to Chile. Her shoulders drooped a bit. It was the story of her life.

"I don't know," she said sadly. "We've got kind of a good-looking new cook at the restaurant, but he only speaks French. I don't know how I could explain the situation to him. I have enough trouble making him understand comments on the cuisine, much less explaining why I want him for a husband."

Picturing how the scene might look, Ross wanted to laugh. "He might take it the wrong way," he warned solemnly.

She nodded. "Yes, I'm afraid he might. And then we might get into areas of husbandom that I don't intend to explore at all."

She said it so vehemently, he wanted to hear more. Those very areas she was disavowing were probably the areas he was becoming more and more interested in every moment he sat beside her.

"What do you mean?" he prompted softly.

She picked up a pillow and plumped it in her lap. "I've already decided that my romantic days are over. That sort of thing only gets in the way of real life. I'm better off without it."

"I see." But he didn't. The woman was alive with a latent sexuality that she couldn't hide. His glance fell to brush across the rise of her peaked breasts against the fluffy knit of the sweater. Something stirred inside him. He realized, with a feeling of wonder, that he wanted her, that he desired her with a hot, rushing sense of masculine joy that he hadn't felt in years.

"No French chef, then," he said, his voice husky with a new awareness.

She reconsidered for a moment, not noticing the change in him. "There would be one real advantage to the French chef. Since he doesn't know how to speak English, he couldn't mess me up with Aunt Doris, even if he tried. All he would be able to do would be to stand around and grin and say, '*Mais oui, madame,*' and things like that. No one would have a clue."

"Unless Aunt Doris speaks French."

Charity sank against the back of the couch, laughing. "Lord, I hadn't thought of that." Her hair flew in wild wisps about her face. She reached up to push it away without annoyance, unconscious of how that gesture arched her body, and not noticing the shudder that went through Ross as he watched.

His mouth was dry. She looked cuddly. Like a slinky teddy bear. Those breasts under that sweater— He could hardly keep from reaching for her. He dug his fingers into the cushion, cursing under his breath. What was the matter with him? He was acting like a teenager. He shifted his position on the couch, moving into the corner, forcing himself to smile. "Better stick with the temporary from the agency," he advised, his voice a hoarse whisper.

She made a face. "The gargoyle?"

Ross straightened, breathing deeply, concentrating on a distant wall. He'd tell her the truth at last and restore some order here. But before he managed to get the words out, there was a knock on the doorframe. A slight, gangly looking young man stood there, his expression intense under a shock of orange hair.

"Yes?" Charity said the word a little impatiently. She was enjoying her conversation with Mason's friend, and she knew there wasn't much time left before he would have to leave for the airport.

"Hi," said the intruder expectantly. "I'm Paul Lomax. You must be Mason's sister Charity."

The air went very still. Charity stiffened, her hands clutching the arm of the couch. She pinned the newcomer with a fierce stare while she slowly digested what he'd said. Then she rose and Ross rose behind her, wishing he had a clever one-liner on the tip of his tongue to save this situation.

"That's right," Charity said slowly, still staring at the newcomer. "Oh. I see." She pointed a finger at him. "You are Paul." She turned the finger in on herself. "And I'm Charity." She turned slowly and glared up at Ross, her tone turning to gravel. "And who are you?"

He shrugged his arms wide and gave her a smile he hoped was ingratiating enough. "Ross Parker," he said. "Your hired husband." He looked hopefully for signs that she saw the joke in all this.

But he looked in vain.

Charity was furious. Suddenly she was aware of just how comfortable she'd been with this man, and all the time he'd been lying to her! She'd said things she never would have told him if she'd realized who he was. "Of all the sneaky, rotten—"

"I tried to tell you. I could hardly get a word in edgewise."

Her eyes sparked. Not only did he trick her, he insulted her as well! "So I talk too much, do I?" she said, her eyes blazing at him. "Listen—" she jabbed a finger at his chest

"—just exactly who are you and what are you doing here?"

Ross caught hold of her hand, his fingers gently circling her wrist. He had an impulse to protect her, but he didn't have the slightest idea what she needed protecting from. "I told you. I was sent over by the agency."

She stared at his hand covering hers, then jerked her hand away, totally ignoring Paul, who still stood in the doorway, looking uncertainly from one of them to the other.

"I think I'll come back later," Paul said, and disappeared into the hall.

Neither Ross nor Charity said goodbye.

"I'm not dumb, you know," she snapped, rubbing her wrist as though to erase the sense of his touch. She looked up at him defiantly. "I look at you and I can see what kind of man you are. You aren't going to try to convince me that you make a career out of playing husband. You don't work for any temporary agency."

Ross had come over with every intention of telling her the entire truth about his motives from the start. Fulfilling the role of husband hadn't loomed large in his scheme of things, though he'd been prepared to follow through if necessary to achieve his goal. Now his instincts told him that this was not the best time to reveal himself fully. A bit of a delaying tactic might work out best in the short run.

"You're absolutely right," he told her hastily. "What I'm doing here is helping my sister out. You see, it's her agency. I happened to answer your call."

He looked so sincere. Charity's anger faded a bit, but she was still wary and a bit unnerved. She was usually so careful. She'd certainly let her guard down this time. Thinking he was a friend of Mason's, she'd acted as though he were practically part of the family. She shouldn't have opened up that way. Her hands were trembling. She didn't often open up to strangers—people who wouldn't understand. It upset her to think she'd let this man see her unprofessional side.

"I thought there was something familiar about your voice," she conceded, hiding her hands in the pockets of her slacks. "You're the one I talked to."

He nodded, noting the move and wondering about it. "You interested me. My sister's agency could use the work. I thought I'd come over and . . ." He shrugged, trying to make light of the situation. "And see if I could get a laugh out of the whole business."

That was the wrong choice of words. Her head snapped up and her dark eyes sparked again. "Very funny. A laugh, is it?" She tossed her golden hair, feeling frazzled, feeling tugged and pulled in all directions at once. Suddenly she was near tears and desperate that no one should know. This was important to her. Was that so hard to understand? This had to do with her family and her place in it. It had to do with her self-image and the way she wanted her family to see her—and a lot of other things she couldn't articulate, not even to herself. "This isn't a joke," she said softly, swallowing hard. Her voice came out sounding little-girl-lonely.

"No, no," he said hastily, stepping closer, surprised by the emotion he could read in her face. She wasn't going to cry, was she? What the hell would he do if she did? "I didn't mean that."

She looked up at him with more reproach than anger, blinking rapidly, swallowing her emotions and calming herself. "Why didn't you say who you were right from the start? I think that was very callous of you to let me ramble on and on when you knew very well. . . Why didn't you tell me from the start?"

"I wish I had," he said simply. He smiled at her, intentionally using the blue-eyed charm that usually worked so well with other women. "You do need a husband," he reminded her softly. "And here I am."

She did need a husband. She hesitated, looking up into his eyes. They were awfully blue. Too blue to look away from. She knew suddenly and with certainty that letting this man into her life was going to be dangerous. She stared at him, searching his gaze, wondering.

"Here you are," she repeated, and then she began to circle Ross, for lack of anything better to do, looking him up and down, everywhere but into those piercing blue eyes. He was awfully good-looking. How could she ever have mistaken him for one of Mason's weird friends?

She stopped, finger to her lips, contemplating, not at all sure what she was going to do. It would be easy to go ahead and hire this... this Ross Parker person. But something told her it wouldn't be particularly bright. "I don't know," she said slowly, half teasing, half serious. "I don't want to overdo it here. I'm not sure Aunt Doris is going to believe I could ever have snagged someone quite so... so..." She waved a hand, unable—or unwilling—to put it into words.

"What's the matter?" He looked down at himself, just a bit nonplussed.

"Not a thing," she admitted, a reluctant smile tweaking the corners of her mouth. "That's just it. You'll overwhelm her."

"I hardly think so," he replied. He glanced up, his eyes narrowed. "I didn't overwhelm you."

That's what you think, she mused as she stepped back and leaned up against the wall, still staring at him. His blue gaze followed her. She examined his straight, dark brows, the rugged jawline, the crispness of the white collar at his strong neck. In her wildest dreams she could not have conjured up a more perfect specimen to fit the ideal of what might please Aunt Doris. He looked intelligent, aware, successful—and damned attractive at the same time. What more could Charity ask for?

"What about it?" he asked when she still hesitated. "Are you going to let me stay and be your husband?"

His saying the word sent a shock through her. "I'm still thinking about it," she said defensively.

His grin was crooked and endearing. "I guess it's come down to a fight between me and the French cook, hasn't it?"

She found herself smiling back. "I guess so."

He took a step closer. "Well, I may not speak French, but I can hold chairs and pour the wine and smile a lot." He shrugged casually. "I mean, isn't that the way husbands operate when aunts come to call?"

His gaze still held hers. "I don't know," she said quickly, pulling at the hem of her sweater. "I'm not sure just what husbands do. I've never had one before."

He took another step closer. "Then we're even," he said softly. "I've never been one before."

Crazy. That was the word that kept sailing through her head. She was crazy to feel this sort of buzzing glow as he came nearer, crazy to think she could live with this man hanging around for the next week, crazy not to send him out the door immediately. This was not at all what she'd planned. She'd envisioned an employee, like the men who worked for her at the restaurant, receiving orders, nodding knowledgeably and proceeding to play the roles she assigned. She knew instinctively that there would be none of that with this man. If he agreed to play her husband, he would be the one supplying the script. She would be reacting, not directing. Was she crazy enough to take a chance at it?

Before she could answer that question, the door burst
open and Mason was back, flushed and swaggering, as
though he'd conquered the town while he was out. "Chile,
here we come," he called out. Then he noticed Ross and a
frown darkened his face. "Hello. Who is this?"

"My gargoyle," she said promptly. "What do you think
of him?"

Mason was stunned. "You're kidding. The guy from the
agency?" He came in and looked Ross up and down as
though he were a store mannequin. "He looks okay to
me."

Charity had a feeling that fate was closing in. "Do you
think Aunt Doris will go for this?" She gestured toward
Ross.

Mason nodded, impressed. "Yeah. He fits my descrip-
tion perfectly." He snapped his fingers. "Book him."

Charity sighed. "He doesn't speak French," she murmured, putting off the inevitable.

"I'll learn," Ross murmured back, smiling like the
Cheshire Cat.

She dropped her gaze, unwilling to risk the buzzing glow
again. "I guess you'll do," she muttered almost regret-
fully.

"Sure he'll do," Mason claimed, throwing out his arms
in a grand gesture. "I'll feel ever so much more comfortable about leaving you with this man than with the gargoyle I was expecting." He stuck out his hand. "Mason
Ames, Charity's brother," he said as they shook. "I guess
we're related now, too."

"Must be." Ross returned the greeting. "I'm Ross
Ca...Parker." Suddenly he realized that he still hadn't told
Charity the whole truth—that he had come not to help her
out, but to talk her into joining his consortium. He had to

do it right away. To delay would only make things worse when he finally did tell her.

He turned toward her, his mouth open, ready to launch into a complete explanation, but the look in her eyes stopped him. She was gazing up at him, her eyes wide, searching. Can I trust you? her gaze seemed to be asking. Are you really what you seem to be? Will you treat me well?

He swallowed and frowned. Not yet, he thought. First things first. He would become irreplaceable as her pretend husband, and when her gratitude was in full flower, then he would tell her.

There was something lacking in that logic, but he didn't want to examine it just now. Instead he responded to Mason's offer of a drink and sank down into the couch, countering Mason's jokes with a few light comments of his own. But all the while, those big brown eyes were haunting him. They were eyes he wouldn't want to betray.

Three

Charity stood in the doorway and surveyed her empire with a certain sense of satisfaction. The Golden Tiger was a thriving restaurant. The lunch crowd had hardly evaporated before the tea crowd began to trickle in. The place was never empty, right up until long after closing when they often had to encourage the last of the lingerers to head for their cars. Her success was partly because the classic menu was good, but also due to the inviting atmosphere. People enjoyed eating at the Golden Tiger. It was as simple as that.

The rest of her success was due to good employees, hard work and attention to detail—and that included the image the owner projected. Instead of the barefoot gypsy of the day before, Charity was a vision of cool professionalism. Her wild hair was tamed into a sleek French twist. Her gunmetal-gray wool suit and rose-petal crepe de chine blouse were muted and classic. Topping it all off were the

tortoiseshell glasses, which added ten years to her age.
Cool. Composed. Capable. That was Charity Ames at
work.

"Wonderful lunch, Miss Ames." The tall, distinguished-looking man nodded amiably as he passed her on
his way out. "As always."

"Thank you, Mr. Vandenberg," she murmured, smiling at the well-known lawyer. "It's always a pleasure to
have you and your colleagues."

The most important people in town patronized her restaurant. She grinned as she thought of it. What would
Alan Grayson think if he could see her now?

She stopped, frowning, and quietly said the name aloud.
"Alan. Alan Grayson." No twinge. No wince. No pain.
Did this mean she was finally over him?

Alan Grayson. Sleek blond hair combed straight back.
A classic profile. Cool gray eyes and an arrogant chin.
She'd been crazy about him, so crazy that she'd opened up
about her life, her family, everything to him. She'd been
there for him at any time of day or night, helping him
through disappointments, soothing his ego when it was
bruised, devoting months to doing nothing but helping him
study for the bar exam, letting him use her apartment when
he ran out of funds. They'd laughed together, loved together. Mutual need had bound them together more and
more tightly, until finally, while they were drinking champagne to celebrate his passing of the bar, she'd blurted out
her dream.

Her dream had involved babies and roses twining over
the garden gate, two cats in the yard—and a wedding ring.
Alan had stared at her, incredulous.

"I can never marry you," he'd told her, as though she
must be blind not to have seen this for herself. "You know
I want to go into politics. I'm aiming high, Charity. You've

got that insane family and too many skeletons in the closet. I'm going to need a wife who can help me get ahead, not one who's an albatross around my neck."

He couldn't understand why that upset her. After all, she'd always been ready to do what was best for him before. This was just another of his demands. "You're flaky, just like your family," he'd said. "No one will ever be able to take you seriously."

That was the last time she'd seen Alan. He'd laughed when she'd told him to leave, but he'd stopped laughing when she'd refused to let him through the door again.

That had been three years ago. She'd heard he was running for the state senate in the fall. Maybe he'd found a suitable wife by now.

She looked out at her restaurant again. Cinnamon-colored banquettes lined the room. Linen tablecloths in burnt orange and waitresses in chocolate brown and russet set the background for countless climbing, trailing and spiraling green plants that seemed to have as much vitality as the diners.

She frowned. Too many plants? No, she decided swiftly. Unlike the way she felt about her apartment, her sense of style for her restaurant was sure and steady. No changes at the moment. This was perfect, just what the clientele wanted. She knew what she was doing, and people took her seriously these days. Alan would be surprised.

Turning with a happy sigh, she went toward her office. Yes, she was satisfied. She had her own restaurant. She was a respected member of the community. She belonged to the chamber of commerce, even if she never made it to the meetings. And now she even had a husband.

A husband!

Just the thought gave her a surge of panic. A husband. Good grief, what had she done?

There was a huge stack of papers on her desk, papers waiting for her signature or approval. But she couldn't be bothered right now. She was too excited. She had a husband. There was actually someone waiting at home for her right now. Before she knew what she was doing, she giggled. Immediately she clapped a hand over her mouth and sank into the chair behind the desk.

Ross had stayed for an hour or so the day before. They'd ironed out some of the details, Charity chattering, avoiding his gaze, Ross quiet, watchful. She'd given him a key, and he'd promised to move in this very afternoon.

"Why don't you let me handle the new decorating scheme," he'd suggested just before leaving. "You won't have the time, and I know a few people who might be helpful."

She'd shrugged, too overwhelmed by what she was getting into to care much about the decor. She had mentioned a figure she wanted to stay within but had otherwise given him carte blanche. Then he'd left and she'd turned to Mason, her eyes wide and wild.

"Am I crazy?" she'd cried. "Did I just give a stranger the key to my apartment?"

Mason had nodded sagely. "No sweat, Char," he'd told her. "The guy's okay. I can tell." Then he'd promptly left for Chile, leaving her to test just how good his judgment was.

But ever since, she'd thought about nothing else. Ross Parker. Her new husband. Every time she let herself think that, a flash of something wild made her tingle.

"It's just a business arrangement," she said aloud to the empty air.

I know that, the empty air seemed to reply. *But who says business can't be fun?*

Her eyes danced behind the huge glasses. She smiled, leaned forward on the desk and began to practice saying wifely things.

She got stuck right away on "Hello, dear, how was your day?" One was supposed to say that when one's spouse came in from work, if she remembered her television families right. But in this case it didn't fit. She was the one coming in from work, and he was the one there waiting for her. So he should be asking her, right?

She frowned. Forget the wifely sayings. She had books to go over, accounts to check. Fixing her glasses more firmly against the bridge of her nose, she settled in, rustling papers and trying to focus her mind.

But it was no use. Her gaze kept straying to the telephone. One little call would let her know for sure whether he was there or not. One little call.

She gritted her teeth and picked up the receiver, punching in her own number with quick stabs.

"Hello." The masculine voice made her jump, even though it was just what she'd hoped to hear.

"Hello," she replied, grinning in spite of herself. "Who is this?"

"Ross Parker," he said promptly. "Ubiquitous and indispensable husband to the lovely and talented Charity Ames. Why do you ask?"

She laughed. Oh yes, it was going to be lovely! "Just to hear you say that, of course. How are things going? Did you bring your things over? Are you all moved in?"

"Why don't you come on home and find out for yourself?"

"Oh, I couldn't do that."

But why not? She hung up, thought about it, then took the evening off, leaving Nancy in charge. Missing the dinner hour was something she rarely did, but tonight she couldn't keep her mind on the restaurant. So she packed up two full servings of Chicken Kiev into Styrofoam boxes and made her way out to her Fiat Spider in the parking lot.

For just a moment she sat behind the wheel. Was this still Charity Ames, she wondered? The same thirty-two-year-old woman who'd decided men weren't worth the bother? The same woman who'd thrown herself completely into her career and been happy to do so? Was this really her, hurrying to the apartment because a man was waiting? If she didn't watch out, she might grow to like things this way.

She started the car with a growing feeling of anticipation. Something was going to happen tonight. Good or bad, it couldn't be stopped now. She was racing toward destiny.

Destiny wasn't a concept that took up much of Ross's thinking time. He usually dealt with the more immediate and mundane. Right now his biggest worry was finding a bar of soap.

Charity's shower was nice and roomy. The hot, stinging water hit his tanned flesh with just enough force to take his breath away, which he liked. But when he felt in the soap dish, there was nothing, not even the tail ends of a well-used bar. And after helping to move furniture all afternoon, he needed some.

He shut off the water and stepped out of the tub, making immediate puddles on her tiled floor. He tried first one cabinet, then another, and then he looked through every drawer, but with no luck.

"Damn," he breathed, looking around the little room, noting the yellow-billed geese dancing across her wall. "Where the hell do women store their soap?"

The kitchen seemed a likely place to look. He didn't bother with a robe. His plan was to dash to the kitchen, grab some dish detergent if there was nothing else and dash back before his skin even had time to register a hint of cold.

Plans were one thing, carrying them through another. The bright kitchen was clean and tidy, but soap was scarce, and the dish detergent wasn't underneath the sink where he'd expected to find it. Shaking his head with exasperation, he decided to return to the bathroom, but before he'd taken more than two steps, someone knocked on the front door.

"Ross?"

It was Charity, back much sooner than he'd expected. Ross looked down at his naked body. "Just a minute," he called, turning toward the bathroom.

"I can't wait! I'm dropping everything! Hurry up and open the door."

The bathroom was all the way on the other side of the apartment. The front door was only a few steps away. Ross hesitated, looking about quickly. Shrugging, he grabbed a dish towel that hung on a rack by the kitchen door. "Coming," he called as he tried to pull the little cloth around his hips.

The day before, Charity had found Ross awfully attractive. She expected to find him so again. She expected to find him handsome and appealing and utterly charming. She did not expect to find him naked. So when the door opened and revealed Ross, tall and tan, dark hair curling tightly around smooth nipples and tapering down to the flattest, most muscular stomach she'd ever seen, she gasped and did, in fact, drop everything she'd held in her arms.

"Here, let me help you," he said, reaching down.

"No!" she shrieked, pushing at him with both hands. There was no way that tiny bit of cloth would stay in place if he bent down, and right now it was exposing a wide section of flank as it was.

He looked a bit startled, but he straightened again. Meanwhile her loud cry had its effect. Doors opened up down the hall. Heads popped out. Wide eyes stared incredulously, and then the grins started to appear.

"Having trouble, Charity?" the gray-haired woman from across the hall asked. She looked Ross over with interest. "Everything all right?"

Charity's cheeks were bright red. This couldn't really be happening to her. This had to be a nightmare. "Oh, yes, certainly," she managed to reply brightly. She smiled up and down the hall to reassure them. "No problem here."

No problem, but a naked man was standing in her doorway, holding a yellow cherry-print cloth over his private parts. She glanced at where his hand still held the corners of the puny thing together, then looked quickly away again. "Get inside," she whispered wildly as she leaned down to pick up the Styrofoam boxes. She rose again, staring at her purse, which still lay at her feet. Both hands were full. Should she drop one box, or just forget the purse was hers?

Ross still stood in the doorway. He hadn't moved an inch. "Let me get it," he said impatiently.

"No, no, no," she urged, still wearing a plastered-on smile for their audience. "Don't you dare!"

One well-placed kick of her foot and the purse went sailing right past him into her apartment. "There, you see? I can handle it myself." She turned for one last smile at her neighbors. "Everything's fine," she called. "Just fine."

The grins were dissolving into giggles. Ross leaned out and waved. "Everything's fine," he said, backing her up. "No problem."

"Get inside," she muttered fiercely through gritted teeth. She pushed in as well, kicked the door closed with her foot, placed the two boxes carefully on an entry table and leaned against the closed door, trying to calm herself, clenching her fists at her sides.

Ross stood before her, feeling ridiculously pleased with the way things were going. It was so unlike him to act this way. Something about Charity made him do it, he realized. "Have you had a rough day?" he asked pleasantly, unconsciously echoing the very lines she'd been practicing only half an hour before.

Charity opened her dark eyes wide and glared at him for all she was worth. If only her heart would stop beating so wildly, she might be able to get out at least one coherent sentence before she killed him. "What are you doing running around naked? Are you some kind of pervert?" she cried at last.

He shrugged with casual nonchalance. "That would depend on your definition of a pervert," he said wisely. "I never thought so. The human body is a beautiful thing. Don't you agree?"

"Oh, no." She stuck out a warning hand, afraid he was going to drop the towel and show her just what he meant right here and now. Not that she didn't agree with him. The human body—especially the one before her at this moment—was most certainly something to behold. The man must work out with weights *and* swim a couple of miles a day, she decided. "No, no, no," she continued quickly. "I do agree that the human body is a beautiful thing, but I've already seen one, thank you."

"Then you know what I mean," he said. His eyes were laughing at her, and that was making her even more furious.

She wouldn't allow herself to smile in return.

"Why?" she snapped out, nodding at his condition.

"The usual reason," he returned. "I was taking a shower."

"Oh?" His hair was wet, but she was suspicious.

"You're out of soap," he went on. "I was searching your kitchen—"

"I stock my soap in the hanging rack beside the shower," she told him evenly.

"Oh." For just a second, he was nonplussed. "I didn't look there." His crooked grin asked for forbearance. "Next time I'll know."

"Who says there's going to be a next time?"

He was finally beginning to realize she was really upset. "What are you so angry about?" he asked, truly puzzled. "Just because your neighbors saw me like this?"

"That's only part of it," she snapped.

"Okay. What's the rest?"

She glared at him. She couldn't possibly tell him that his incredibly rugged physique was disturbing her, that it scared her to feel this way about a man she hardly knew, a man she'd hired to live with her. Instead of answering, she gave him her cold look, the one she reserved for employees who were about to be fired. "Get rid of that ridiculous towel and put some clothes on," she ordered frostily.

Ross didn't like being ordered. His blue eyes flashed returning fire as he glared for just a moment. "Fine," he said sharply. "Anything you say." Turning crisply, he snapped the towel off, letting it fly across the room. He was completely naked as he walked away from her.

"Oh!" she cried, itching to throw something at him. But she didn't look away until he'd disappeared into the bathroom.

And then she looked at her apartment. She'd given Ross a free hand in redecorating. She'd assumed he would bring in a few new throw rugs and pictures for the walls, a potted plant or two. Instead, he'd completely gutted her apartment. What she saw staggered her. It was moments before she could speak.

Gone was old the blue sectional couch. Gone were the sculptures and the blue paintings. Instead, elegance and splendor met her gaze. Chippendale? Queen Anne? Regency? She wasn't sure what you called it. But it was everywhere. Mahogany buffed to satiny smoothness was set off against brocade in armchairs, a love seat, low tables and a writing desk. French Impressionist reproductions covered the walls. A Persian rug lay on the livingroom floor. And in the corner a huge china cabinet sat empty.

"What on earth?" she managed to gasp, turning slowly to gaze at each piece. "What's happened?"

Ross was back, dressed in soft gray slacks and carrying a shirt he was about to don. "No rattan," he said. "No grass mats. Nothing tropical."

"No." Her voice sounded like a strangled gasp for air. Nothing tropical. Nothing even remotely middle-class. Where could he possibly have found these things? Was the Queen of England having a rummage sale?

Ross frowned. "Don't you like it?" he asked. He was beginning to get a bad feeling about this. Charity looked like a different woman today. He'd spent the night thinking about her, about her springlike freshness, about her open honesty, her beautiful smile. But the woman he'd been imagining looked nothing like this. The Charity that stood before him looked prim and proper as the old-fashioned stereotype of a town librarian.

He'd thought she looked like a South Sea Islands beauty, but she'd rejected that, so he'd gone to the opposite extreme. He'd called Bernie, a dealer he'd often worked with in the past, and put in a rush order. Bernie owed him a favor or two, and he'd had the best pieces in his warehouse delivered within hours of Ross's call. He'd thought she'd be pleased.

She looked around again. Two bright spots of color highlighted her cheeks. The room was much too lovely. "What showroom did you steal this stuff from?" she snapped.

His eyes narrowed and his hands went to his hips, resting loosely against the belt line. "Don't worry—" he began icily.

She cut him off, glaring at him. "The money I gave you couldn't possibly cover this!" A sweep of her hand told him just what she thought of the entire affair.

His face hardened. He'd expected excitement, delight and, most of all, gratitude. "It's only rented," he assured her. "I've got a friend in the business; don't worry about the cost."

"I want to see receipts." Her voice was that of an employer used to telling others what to do.

"Don't worry about it," he replied, and his voice was that of one unused to doing what someone else told him to. "I've got it covered."

She met his gaze and held it, her own fierce and wary, his dark with anger. What had she been thinking of? He really was a stranger, after all. He was someone she'd hired. She had to maintain the cool, bosslike presence with him, just as she did with her employees at the restaurant. She'd been acting like a little girl getting ready to play house. What a fool!

"You had a call from the relief society, asking for donations," he told her casually. "And your mail is on the entry-hall table."

She was in no mood to look through letters.

"I brought home some dinner," she said evenly, holding up the Styrofoam containers. "Let's eat in the kitchen." Tomorrow it would all go back.

"Fine," he said.

They glared at each other for a long moment, and then she turned abruptly and stalked to the kitchen, pausing only a moment to gasp at the new crystal chandelier hanging from her ceiling. He followed. Once in the kitchen, she hesitated, tempted to slap the Styrofoam container at his place on the little kitchen table, but she couldn't quite do it. Whirling, she took down two china plates and overturned the packages onto them. Pulling silverware out of the drawer, she turned to find Ross already seated, like a typical man, waiting to be served.

"What would you have done if I hadn't brought dinner home?" she asked as she set the food before him. "Starved?"

His blue eyes were coolly assessing. "I hired on here as a husband, not a servant," he reminded her. "My ideas of what a husband deserves may be outdated; I don't know. Perhaps we should go over them and see."

Despite the antagonism that had flared between them, his sensual suggestion made her glare at him, just to show him he was barking up the wrong tree if he had any thoughts along *those* lines.

A bottle of wine stood on the kitchen counter. They each eyed it surreptitiously now and then, but neither made a move to open it. Eating with the man was one thing,

Charity thought to herself. But drinking wine with him was somehow a shade too personal.

She was furious and not really sure just why. Yes, the furniture was all wrong, but so what? In the morning she'd have it all shipped to where it came from, and the incident would be over. Still her emotions were churning, and she could hardly stand to look Ross in the eye without throwing daggers. Why was she feeling such resentment over such a small thing? Was it because he'd disappointed her or because she felt he'd misread her so badly? Was it something else altogether?

She'd been looking forward to this evening. All afternoon she'd been walking on air, thinking about what fun it was going to be to have a make-believe husband. But when she'd come home and faced the genuine article, everything had fallen apart.

She glanced up at him. His face was bland, emotionless. He didn't seem to care about a thing, she decided, feeling even more resentment. She regretted hiring him in the first place. Deliberately she lowered her eyes and stared at the Chicken Kiev that she could hardly taste.

Ross watched her. His anger had already evaporated. He'd guessed wrong about the decorating, that was certain. Somehow he'd threatened her in a way he didn't understand. That could all be rectified if she would only be willing to meet him halfway. He sat back in his chair and watched her eat. It was the prim suit and the hair plastered against her head that way, he decided. Not to mention the glasses that she'd forgotten to take off before coming in. If he could just get back the warm, laughing woman he'd met here the day before, everything would be all right.

"Good dinner," he said at last, putting down his silverware and wiping his mouth with a napkin.

"You can thank the French chef for that," she said crisply, not looking up.

It was on the tip of his tongue to make a sarcastic remark, but he bit it back. Winning this argument would lose him the war. Funny how he cared more than he'd have thought possible that the war not be lost.

"It was good, anyway," he said quietly, then rose and cleared his own place, washing his utensils in the sink.

She watched him when she was sure he wasn't looking. He seemed so large at her sink. She gave up on the food. Ross might think it good, but she couldn't taste it at all. He stood back while she cleaned up after herself. Neither of them said a word for long moments at a time.

"Well," she said brusquely, drying her hands on a cloth. "I guess I'll get to bed."

"Already?" He was taken by surprise. "But it's only—"

"I'm really tired." She almost tried to smile at him. "Maybe after a good night's sleep I'll be able to put all this in better perspective."

He raised an eyebrow. "Don't you think we should discuss what we're going to do once your aunt gets here? Don't you think we should go over a game plan?"

"Tomorrow." She put a hand to her head. A headache was threatening. "We'll do that tomorrow." She looked at him. His gaze was midnight blue and impenetrable, but still she felt vulnerable—as though he could read her mind. "I . . . I'm sorry I flew off the handle," she said grudgingly. "But the furniture . . ."

"Is impossible." He smiled at her. "I can see that now."

She felt relief wash through her body. "Yes. We'll have to send it back."

"Of course."

She felt like a fool, and here he was being so adult about everything. All she could think of was escape from his searching gaze. "Well, good night," she said again, turning away. She walked into her room and stopped, hand to her throat. There was a suitcase open on the floor. Men's shirts spilled out of it. A pair of men's slacks was flung across her bed. He'd moved in. This man—this *stranger*— was invading her bedroom!

She spun. "What—why?"

Ross had followed her to the doorway. He watched her reaction with a mixture of amusement and consternation. If only he could figure out what was bothering her so much. "Aunt Doris will find it peculiar if we don't share a bedroom, don't you think?"

Charity squared her shoulders. She knew she was overreacting, but she just couldn't help it. She wasn't used to seeing men's things strewed all over her room. It had been a long time since any man had visited her bedroom. She wasn't prepared for this just now. "Aunt Doris isn't here yet," she reminded Ross icily. "Until she arrives, you sleep in the guest room." And I'll think of some way to get out of this by then, she promised herself silently.

Ross stared at Charity, resisting the urge to shake some sense into her. For all her imperiousness, there was a softness in her that she tried to deny. Suddenly he knew something he'd never been told. Life had not been totally kind to Charity. She was guarded, protective. How had she been hurt?

He shook his head, astonished at **his** own feelings. He didn't remember ever noticing something like this about a woman before. He usually shied away from complications. He didn't know why women seemed to take life so seriously. Life was a game played best by those who could stay the most detached. But for some reason, this time he couldn't turn from his feelings. This time he wanted to brush away the wariness he could see in the depths of her warm brown eyes—brush it away as he would wipe away a crust of cobwebs from a lovely painting so that he could better enjoy its beauty.

"All right," he said gruffly. "I'll get my things out of here."

She hid in the bathroom while he cleaned away his clothes, waiting until he left the room before she came out. She slipped out of her suit and into a long green-cotton nightgown, then snuggled deep into her covers, squinting her eyes closed and praying for sleep. But she might as well have prayed for the moon.

The headache that had been threatening came on full force. Her head was pounding like the surf on jagged rocks. She couldn't think straight, she couldn't plan what she was going to do about Ross Parker—and she certainly couldn't sleep.

Finally she gave up, turned on her light and stared at the ceiling. She couldn't go on this way. Listening very carefully, she couldn't detect a sound from the rest of the apartment. Maybe he'd gone to bed, too. Maybe she could risk a foray into the kitchen to get herself some aspirin.

Slipping silently from the bed, she walked softly to the door and opened it a crack. There was no light on in the living room or kitchen. She opened the door all the way and stood very still, listening intently and staring out into the darkness.

Though she couldn't see him, Ross was sitting in that darkness. He'd turned off all the lights and then sunk down into one of the Regency chairs to think things over. What the hell was he doing here, anyway? He had a very large urge to pack up and go back to his own comfortable beach condominium.

Then he heard a noise, and when he looked up he saw Charity silhouetted in the doorway of the bedroom. She stood with the light at her back, and her loosened hair floated around her shoulders like spun gold. He couldn't see her face, but her long cotton nightgown was just thin enough to let light through so he could see all the rest of her clearly. Her legs were long and silky, her hips round and her full breasts peaked with hard, dark tips. His stomach turned over as he watched her. Hot, surging desire coursed through him. Suddenly he realized why he was staying here, and it didn't have anything to do with his consortium.

"Hi," he said into the darkness, making her jump. But she didn't retreat into the bedroom. Instead she focused in the dark until she could see him.

"I was just going for aspirin," she said.

"Headache?"

"Yes."

He rose. "I've got a better idea. Let's share that bottle of wine."

"Oh, I don't think so...."

He erased the distance between them with a few quick strides. She stood paralyzed as he took her hand.

"Come on," he said softly, looking down into the wide eyes. "We're supposed to be husband and wife. We've got to get more used to each other, or she'll never buy it. Come have a drink. Relax. Let's get to know each other."

She knew he was right. It was something they had to do to be convincing. But she wasn't afraid of getting to know him or of his getting to know her. It was knowing herself that scared her most.

She nodded. "Okay," she said softly, letting him lead her to the kitchen. Her heart was beating as though he were leading her to her doom.

Four

Just one glass," she said firmly when she first sat beside him on the brocade couch.

Of course, one glass led to another, and the headache began to fade. Ross started to look rather benign sitting in the light of the single lamp, and before Charity knew what was happening, she'd slid down to sit on the floor, saying, "This elegant upholstery makes me nervous. I know I'm going to spill wine all over it." She leaned against the coffee table and he slid down next to her, a bit stiffly at first. He loosened up as he realized how comfortable it really was, and before long they were talking like cautious friends instead of sparring partners.

"What I don't understand," Ross said at last, when the bottle was empty and another had been found in a kitchen cabinet, "is why a woman like you hasn't been married before. For real, I mean."

That statement might have raised her hackles an hour or so earlier, but now she was relaxed enough to take it casually. She smiled, leaning her chin into the cup of her hand, her elbow on the coffee table. "And here I thought you were a perceptive man," she teased. "You said it yourself. My style is South Sea Islands, no matter how much I try to hide it."

He raised an eyebrow, his dark gaze skimming across her flyaway hair and the nightgown that she had unconsciously allowed to drape provocatively off one shoulder. "South Sea Islands is damned alluring," he said flatly. "If you think that's turning men off, you're wrong."

"That's not what I mean." She took another sip of golden wine, completely unaware of the seductive picture she made beside him. "It's just that it seems to turn the *wrong* men on. I always end up being someone's outlet." She stared at Ross. She'd never told anyone this sort of thing before, and yet it just rolled out for him. What was it about this man that made her feel so vulnerable and at the same time so free?

His skeptical frown told her he still didn't understand. "Take Freddy Wainehold," she went on, narrowing her eyes to look into the past. "A stockbroker. Staid. Boring even. We met when I was trying out restaurant management, working as an assistant manager at the Mellow Prawn in Beverly Hills. He asked me out. We seemed to get along just fine. He even asked me to marry him. And—" she shrugged, unable to believe it herself now "—I actually considered doing just that at the time. And then I began to realize a disturbing pattern was emerging." She looked at Ross over the rim of her glass. "All our dates ended up at the circus."

Ross looked blank. "At the circus?"

She nodded. "Down in the Los Angeles area, you can always find the circus playing somewhere. And we did. He just loved the circus. He would sit on the edge of his seat until the clowns came out, and then he would roar with laughter at everything they did." She grinned. "The poor guy didn't want to be a stockbroker at all. He wanted to be a circus clown. Only he couldn't really admit it to anyone, and the closest he could come was by marrying me."

"You?" Ross put down his glass with a thump as if the very idea offended him. "Don't be absurd."

Charity was beyond resenting it. She'd accepted certain things about her life, which was why her success with her restaurant was so important to her. It told her she could stand on her own, that she didn't need a man in her life to survive. Despite her kooky background, she could make it in the serious world.

"It's true," she told Ross, smiling a little. "There's something unconventional deep down inside me, and certain people sense it. They don't dare do unconventional things themselves, but dating me makes them feel as though they're living dangerously." Her smile broadened and her soft eyes shone. He almost hooted to think that she could be dangerous to anyone. "I know you don't believe me, but it's true. It took me years to figure this out."

He glared at her. "I hate to break this to you, Charity Ames," he said with a bite in his voice. "But you're just not that weird." He waved his hand dismissingly. "Lovely, yes. A little wild, perhaps. Unconventional. Impetuous. Okay. But you're not a kook. You're not crazy. And you're certainly not scary."

Charity threw back her head and laughed. "See what a good job I'm doing of hiding it?" she chortled.

For reasons he himself couldn't fathom, Ross didn't find it at all amusing. "You seem like a mature woman to me," he went on gruffly. "You run your own life, your own restaurant—"

"And that's important." She shook a finger at him. "My restaurant. My symbol of independence." She took another long sip of wine and frowned. "Have you ever heard of a man named Ross Carpenter?" she asked.

He looked at her quickly, but her eyes were guileless. "I've heard of him," he said carefully. "Why?"

"Then I guess you know he's one of these magicians who takes a seedy shopping area under his wing and, with a bit of face-lifting and a lot of phony P.R. work, turns it into a trendy mall where the city's finest meet and greet."

Ross squirmed. He wanted nothing more than to defend himself and his work from her scathing denouncement, but he bit his tongue and kept still.

"He's in the process of doing exactly that out on the Dos Pueblos Pier where I have my restaurant," she went on. "He's been after me for months to join his consortium. All the others on the pier have joined."

"Why not join up?" he said, staring at his wine. "I hear he's had a lot of success with his methods."

She nodded. "Yes, he has. But if I joined, I would be part of something else. Can you understand that? The Golden Tiger wouldn't be *me* any longer. I couldn't claim to have brought about success on my own, and that's very important to me." She shrugged. "I'd rather sell out than buy in." She smiled, pleased with the wording she'd used.

Ross frowned. That was the attitude he'd come to fight. Funny how he didn't seem to have any interest in counter-attack at the moment. His mind was too full of her and her attractions. Her hair, he noticed, was the color of champagne. Her eyes were dark and full of shadows. "Well, why didn't you marry one of these daredevils who used

you to court danger?'' he said, changing the subject back
again.

"Oh no." She sobered, her eyes darkening even more.
"There always came a time when they found out about the
rest of my family, and then they backed away fast. A little
daring is one thing. Total pandemonium is another.''

She made him smile, even when he wasn't sure what he
was smiling about. "Tell me about the others.''

"Let's see." Her brow furled in thought. "There was
Hugh Crest who thought he was quite a free spirit because
he'd had his hair permed. And Ted Arnold who was really
a darling. But he still lived with his mother, and when she
took a trip to Hawaii and met *my* mother, it was all over.''

"Your mother's in Hawaii?''

She used her finger to wipe up a bit of moisture on the
table and nodded. "Yes. She's lived there since my father
died about eight years ago. She reads palms and tarot
cards.'' Her quick, brittle smile couldn't completely hide
the mixed feelings she still had for her mother. "Don't ever
go to her. All she ever foresees are long trips which will end
in unhappiness and mysterious packages which will arrive
on your doorstep.'' She laughed softly. "Those she will
advise you to burn before opening. The trips she will advise you to avoid at all costs. If you listen to her, you'll
never have any fun at all.''

The next logical topic was Alan, of course. His handsome face flashed into her mind, but she blinked him away.
She was completely over him, but it still hurt. She didn't
want to talk about that failed romance. She'd been telling
Ross things that were close enough to the quick as it was.
Enough was enough. Quickly she turned the conversation
to Ross.

"How about you?'' she asked brightly. "Why aren't you
married? And who was special in your life?''

"Me?" He thought for a moment and tried to recall some special lady, someone he might almost have married. He thought harder, suddenly aghast. There wasn't one woman who stood out from the others. How could that be? After all the years, all the women? Lovely faces, lovely bodies. Was that all there was? Nothing to differentiate one from another? He'd never realized it before, but there was no one. What was wrong with him?

"I've been too busy," he muttered evasively, refilling both their glasses with the shimmering liquid.

"Doing what?" she prompted.

He stared at her. Here it was again, another opening to tell her who he really was. His gaze flickered over her trusting face, the soft hair that fell in disarray about her shoulders, the clinging cloth that outlined her breasts, and he knew he wasn't going to jeopardize this feeling that was growing between them by telling her the truth right now. Guilt twinged sharply, but he ignored it.

"All the wrong things, obviously," he said instead of explaining. He lifted his glass, meeting hers in a toast. "Here's to our marriage," he said, his voice low, husky and aware. "May it be short . . . and sweet."

She laughed and clinked her glass against his, but when their eyes met, the laughter died in her throat. She recognized the male hunger she read in his eyes. She'd seen it before without feeling overwhelmed. Manipulating men away from the brink was a fine talent she'd developed over the years, and she was usually fairly confident of her ability to avoid unpleasantness.

This was a little different. For some strange reason, her pulse was pounding. Something was fluttering inside her, throwing her off her stride. She carefully placed the wineglass down on the table and spread her flattened hands against the cool wood, staring at them.

"I guess we ought to talk about the job," she said, her voice suddenly prim and businesslike. "About just what you'll be doing."

"If you'd like." Amusement colored his tone. She glanced at him sharply. There was no laughter evident in his eyes, but she went on.

"The first thing you've got to understand is that Aunt Doris is sort of a rigid person. She likes things done right. She cares about honesty, integrity and good table manners, in that order." She sighed, feeling better now that she was back on firm ground, and she looked up at Ross. "How does that fit in with your plans?"

He took a slow sip, but his gaze didn't leave her face. "Well, the honesty goes without saying." He felt another twinge of guilt, but what could he do? "The integrity—I think I can stand on my reputation there. The good table manners I could work on."

She looked relieved. "Could you? I know it's hard for people who haven't been brought up that way."

He grinned. "What makes you think I wasn't brought up with good manners?"

"Oh! I didn't mean…" She reached out and touched his arm. That was a mistake. His flesh felt warm and alive under the crisp fabric of his shirt. She pulled her hand back quickly. "Listen, I'm the one who wasn't brought up with good manners. I wasn't brought up with any manners at all. I lived in thatched huts all over the South Pacific as a child. I spent most of my toddling years careening about the reef, reaching out my chubby little hands for the bright fishes in the lagoons. What do I know about manners? The only thing I have going for me is common sense, and that's never good enough for Aunt Doris."

Ross shifted his position, thrusting his long legs out under the table and leaning against the couch. Through sheer luck, that brought him even closer to where Charity was sitting, but she didn't notice in time to do anything about it. When he turned toward her again, she could feel his breath stir her hair.

"What would be good enough for Aunt Doris?"

Charity smiled. "To have us all normal. To have me married to a doctor, Faith married to a lawyer and Mason married to a debutante. To have all of us, with assorted tiny tots, living with her in one great big house outside of Boston. Sort of *Dallas*-the-TV-show-style, you know what I mean? She'd be Miss Ellie, the glue that holds us all together." She sighed. "She'll never get that, and she knows it. So I'd like her to have something, you know? I'd like her to think that at least one of us turned out the way she tried to direct us."

"Why does it matter so much what Aunt Doris thinks?" he asked, searching her face.

He still didn't understand? "I love her," she said simply.

He frowned. He loved people, too, he supposed. His mother. His sister. But he never *did* things to please them just because he loved them. In some ways this was a new concept to him. Giving instead of taking as though it were one's due.

"She's so good," Charity was saying, still trying to explain. "And she tries so hard." She hesitated, knowing Ross still didn't fully understand and determined that he should, no matter what it cost to convince him. "You see, she took the three of us in, my sister and Mason and me, when..." She took a deep breath. This was the hard part. This was what she fought so hard to hide, to run from. Now she was actually going to tell Ross. She'd hardly ever told anyone, but she was going to tell this make-believe husband. "When my parents went to prison," she said quickly, getting it over with.

"Prison?" Startled, he couldn't disguise the shock in his voice.

"Yes." She raised her chin, her eyes clear and challenging. "Eighteen months for running an illegal lottery in Tonga." There. She'd said it. She hadn't said it often, though it had happened years ago. But it was time to face it, to put the past behind her. She was proud of herself for the way she'd laid it out on the table, but for some reason she couldn't force herself to meet Ross's gaze again. Suddenly she just wanted to leave the room.

"Would you like some crackers or something else to eat?" she said shakily, reaching out to get a handhold to pull herself up from. "I could just run to the kitchen and—"

His hands were on her shoulders, pulling her against him. "I don't want any crackers," he said. She felt slender and fragile, and he pulled her closer.

She curled against his chest, her control shattered for the moment. He felt unbelievably protective. She wanted to close her eyes and melt into his embrace and stay that way forever. He was stroking her hair. There was a lump rising in her throat.

"I can't let Aunt Doris down," she told him, her voice muffled by his soft shirt. "She tried so hard and got so little in return."

"We won't let her down," he said. His hand cupped her cheek. She seemed as vulnerable as a captured bird, soft and warm and uncertain. A hot sense of possession spread through him. "We'll make her happy. Trust me."

Charity smiled, her face pressed against his chest, tears trembling in her eyes. "The thing that terrifies me most is,

once she gets here, I'm going to have to cook. Real meals."
She tried to laugh, but the sound was choked in her throat.

Ross felt shaken. All these years of hip encounters with
sophisticated women were swept away. Something about
Charity Ames brought out raw emotion in him, brought
him back to a primal level where he wanted to flex his
muscles and growl. Her body was so sweet in the wispy
cloth. His hand slid down from her hair, cupped her
shoulder, then found her breast, and as his fingers curled
about the lovely curve, he felt something twist inside him,
something catch at his breath.

"Don't touch me," she whispered, though she didn't
pull away.

"Then don't be so touchable," he whispered back. But
reluctantly he drew his hand back. She turned her head and
looked up at him. Her dark eyes, wide with wonder, were
shadowed by strands of wild hair that fell down from her
forehead. Like a startled deer peering out through a bed of
forest ferns, he thought a bit irrationally. Her red lips were
slightly open, as though she were about to warn him again,
but no words came. He felt a surge of desire so strong, it
shook him hard. He had to get back, get away from her,
before he did something.

"Charity," he said warningly, using his hands to set her
a bit away. He'd meant to go on, to speak sternly, to build
a quick wall of formality between them, but he never got
the chance.

She turned to look at him again, going to her knees. Her
eyes were as mysteriously dark as a midnight sky. Bracing
herself with one hand on the couch, the other on the edge
of the coffee table, she leaned toward him. His stern speech
died in his throat as her mouth found his. Only their lips
touched, but heat poured into him. She was smooth as
butter, sweeter than the wine they'd been drinking, and

when her tongue flickered against his lips, he groaned,
moving involuntarily, aching with the need to take her
body with his own.

But something held him back. This was her kiss. Just her
mouth touched his. Then as she leaned closer, the tips of
her breasts touched his chest. Her lips parted and he sank
into her mouth, arching to press more firmly against her
breasts, clutching handfuls of carpet and brocade to keep
from using his hands in a way that might frighten her.

But then she was pulling back, her breath coming in
gasps, her hands to her face. "I'm sorry," she choked out.
"Oh, Lord, I'm so sorry." She peeked at him through
spread fingers. "I never should have done that. I didn't
mean to imply...to make you think..."

His overpowering urge was to rip away her nightgown
and make her admit she wanted him as much as he wanted
her. The kiss had said it all. A momentary rage surged
through him at her denial, but he fought the primitive im-
pulses. The last thing in the world he wanted to do was to
hurt her in any way. Instead of answering her, he leaned
against the couch, his eyes tightly closed, his hands balled
into fists, waiting until he could think clearly again.

"Ross?" she asked tentatively.

He grunted, not opening his eyes.

"I'm really, really sorry. That was exactly what I wanted
to avoid, and then I was the one who went ahead and did
it."

He opened one eye and looked at her. "Why?" he
growled.

"Why? Why what?" She frowned.

"Why did you do it?" He opened both eyes and
straightened to face her. "Come on, Charity," he coaxed
softly. "You just gave me the most seductive kiss I've ever

had." He shrugged. "You wish you hadn't done it. I'll accept that. But I want you to say it."

She looked completely uncomfortable. "Say what?"

"Why you did it." He fixed her with a savage glare. "Come on, Charity. Give."

She opened her mouth, then closed it again and avoided his eyes. "I did it because . . . because . . ." She took a deep breath. "Because I wanted to." She glanced at him sideways, then quickly looked away again. "Because you look so good," she admitted, her voice hardly loud enough to be heard. "Because you feel so good. Because I feel so good when you touch me."

His face relaxed in a long, slow smile. "Right," he murmured, reaching out to thread his fingers through her wild hair. "My turn." His fingers tightened and he pulled her toward him.

She melted against him. Her mouth was his, and he took it as he meant to take the rest of her. The hard insistence of his probe was softened by his need to pleasure her as well as himself. His hand took her breast again, and this time she sighed and stretched to his touch, crying out softly when he dragged his thumb across the nipple. The nightgown slipped easily up above her hips, and there was only the scrap of nylon beneath. His hand flattened over her smooth stomach, then lowered to pull away that last barrier.

"No! Oh no," she cried, rolling away from his touch. "Don't, Ross. We can't."

He pulled her back into his arms, kissing her hair, her forehead, her lips.

"Charity, Charity," he murmured. "I want to make love with you. I want to touch you and I want you to touch me. I want to start a fire inside you that only I can quench." He took her chin in his hand. "Don't pretend you don't want that, too."

"No, Ross." She shook her head, her dark eyes pleading for him to understand. "I can't sleep with you."

He didn't take her seriously at first. "Why not?" He grinned. "We're married, aren't we?"

She nodded. "That's just it. This whole marriage farce. That's why we can't."

His eyes darkened. He was beginning to realize she was serious. And stubborn. "That doesn't make any sense."

"I knew you wouldn't understand."

He took a deep breath. "I'm trying very hard to understand." But he reached for her again.

"We shouldn't do this," she whispered.

"Why not?" he murmured, pushing back her hair and nuzzling his face against her hairline.

But Charity didn't melt against him this time. "It's wrong. This whole thing is wrong. We're insulting the entire institution of marriage. Don't you see?"

"No, I don't see." His voice was hard, angry, but at the same time he was watching her, and he knew she was sincere. She really meant it. She couldn't follow the urgency her body demanded because of some sort of abstract loyalty to the idea of marriage.

He could probably talk her out of it.

Then he had a wild impulse to ask her to marry him for real. Anything. Anything at all. And then he frowned, trying to remember why he'd come here in the first place.

The consortium. That was it. He needed her restaurant to join.

That motivation seemed an aeon away. All he wanted now was her body, her soul, her heart. Her heart? He swallowed hard and rose to pace across the room. He was getting carried away. He'd never given up a thing before in order to get a woman when he wanted her. This was no time to set a precedent.

"Charity," he began, moving toward her.

Her head came up with a snap. "No," she said firmly, her mouth set. "This is all wrong. It has been from the start. We can't pretend to be married. We can't try to fool Aunt Doris." She rose, her spine stiff, her face determined. "I'll call her in the morning, tell her the truth." She glanced at him as though she hardly knew him. "You can spend the night, if you like. But you'll have to leave first thing in the morning." He watched, speechless, as she took the last few measured steps to her bedroom. "Good night," she said primly. "I'm sorry I've caused you all this bother. I'll have a check ready before you go." Her glance was cool, distant. "Good night," she said again, and disappeared, closing the door firmly behind her.

Ross watched, stunned. When she decided to turn into the ice maiden, she did a damn good job of it. He didn't know whether to be angry or to laugh out loud. He looked at the two empty wineglasses sitting on the coffee table. How could something so good have slipped out of his grasp so quickly? He shook his head and strode to the spare bedroom, glad to see he did have a bathroom of his own there. He was going to need a cold shower, and need it fast.

Five

————

A calliope played a deafeningly cheery tune. Charity pushed her way through a room full of balloons and cotton candy until she came to the rope ladder. Up she climbed, higher and higher, to the very top of the big-top tent. She stepped out onto the tiny platform, and across the way she could see Ross, grinning. She smiled and lifted her arms, suddenly exultant. And then she was flying through the air, her fingers wrapped tightly around the bar of the trapeze. She swung across the wide expanse, once, twice, three times, and then she let go, sailing through space, her body arched like a bird's.

Ross was waiting for her, his muscular legs wound about the ropes of his own trapeze, his arms stretched toward her. She reached for him. Their fingers almost touched.

"Charity!"

But no, it was wrong! Ross's hands slipped out of her grasp and she wanted to scream. She was falling . . . falling. . . .

"Charity!"

She came to earth with a thump, her dream splintering around her. That voice. She knew that voice.

"Charity, darling, wake up. It's me, Aunt Doris."

Charity blinked sleepy eyes and wished to heaven that she were still dreaming. "Aunt Doris?" she repeated blearily.

"Yes, dear. Didn't you get my letter? I decided to come early, and here I am."

Charity tried to smile. Yes, there she was. Good old Aunt Doris, her gray hair frizzing comfortably about her weathered face, her sensible cardigan about her shoulders, her classic plaid wool skirt, her sensible shoes. And right behind her stood Ross.

At least he'd had the decency to don a pair of baggy pajama bottoms. But his chest was bare. And he looked gorgeous. Not like a husband at all, more like a . . . Charity groaned and closed her eyes, wanting to sink down into the covers and stay there.

"Come along, dear," Aunt Doris was saying brusquely. "It's not like you to be such a slugabed. Do you realize it's almost ten o'clock? What on earth were you up to last night to make you sleep so late? Why, when you lived with me, you were always the first one up. Do you remember how you used to surprise me by fixing breakfast before anyone else was awake?"

The only incident that Charity could recall involved hideously burned toast and incredible, rubbery eggs, but she nodded as though fixing breakfast had been her main occupation in those days. "I'm sorry I wasn't up to greet you," she murmured dutifully, reaching up to accept the

woman's affectionate hug and completely forgetting that
as a restaurant owner who seldom got home from work
before midnight, she had every excuse to sleep late.

She glared at Ross over Aunt Doris's shoulder, wondering why he was standing there grinning like an idiot. Had
Aunt Doris seen him yet? Why didn't he take this opportunity to sneak out the back way and set her free from ex-
planations that promised to be embarrassing at best? Her
mind was beginning to clear, and memories of the night
before came flooding back. She'd decided not to lie to
Aunt Doris, hadn't she? And now here was Ross, ruining
everything.

Go! she mouthed at him.

No, he mouthed back, still grinning.

Aunt Doris released her. "I've met your husband,
Charity," she said, shattering her last hope. "And I must
tell you how pleased I am." Doris turned and motioned for
Ross to join them. Charity's heart sank. All her good intentions were down the drain. If Ross had already identi-
fied himself as her husband, how could she contradict
him? The whole ugly story would come out, and things
would be that much worse. She'd have to bluff her way
through this and then send Ross on his way. What would
she tell Aunt Doris? Something would come to mind. It
had to.

"Now, I want a picture of the two of you together,"
Doris was saying. Charity stiffened as Ross slipped down
on the bed beside her, reaching out to tousle her hair affectionately.

"Yes, Char and I are quite happy together," he said,
looking like the cat that ate the canary. "You won't find
another couple like us."

"That's for sure," Charity replied a bit more causti-
cally than necessary. She was bristling at his use of the
nickname only Mason ever used. "We're unique."

"Get closer, now," Aunt Doris said, her eye to the
viewfinder.

"The closer the better," Ross murmured, putting an arm
around Charity's shoulders and drawing her near.

The hand she threw out to stop him connected with the
wiry hair of his muscular chest, and she pulled it back immediately.

"Say 'cheese,'" Aunt Doris cried from behind the
camera.

"Say 'goodbye,'" Charity whispered to Ross from behind teeth clenched into a semblance of a smile. "You've
got to get out of here."

"Too late," he said back, his own smile even wider and
much more realistic.

"There." Aunt Doris snapped the picture, and the flash
nearly blinded them both. "Now I've got to run down and
see if the taxi man has unloaded my luggage." Doris strode
purposefully toward the door. "I won't be but a minute,
dears," she called cheerfully before she disappeared.

"You—" Charity turned on Ross the moment her aunt
had left.

"Me," he agreed happily, bending down to kiss the tip
of her nose before she could protect herself. "I get to be
your husband after all. I couldn't help it. There she was at
the door, and there I was answering the door in my paja-
mas. What was I supposed to do—tell her I was merely
your guest for the night?"

"But we'd decided not to lie."

"You decided. I've always been for it." He slipped out
of bed. "I'm going to clean my stuff out of the spare bed-

room before she gets back. We don't want her thinking the happy couple is sleeping apart, do we?''

Charity groaned and hid her face in her pillow while Ross left the room. He was whistling, which made her gnash her teeth. Destiny seemed to have taken a hand, and she didn't see that there was much she could do about it for the moment.

She dressed quickly, pulling on a sweatshirt and blue jeans. She ran a brush through her hair but ignored makeup. Emerging from her bathroom, she found Ross climbing into a pair of slacks. Instead of retreating as she would normally have done, she stood in the doorway and watched, her hands on her hips, just to emphasize that she wasn't pleased with the way things were turning out, and that she wasn't about to concede the stewardship of this project to him.

"Think I need a shirt?" he asked wryly, reading her motives and not beyond teasing her.

"I think you need a keeper," she snapped, wishing she didn't like the view of his naked chest quite so much.

"Exactly," he agreed, reaching into one of the many piles he'd made on her bedroom floor and pulling out a soft sea-green polo shirt. "That's why I decided to go ahead and marry you."

"We are not married," she said evenly, watching him stick his arms in the armholes, raise the shirt over his head and then get his head caught in the neck because he hadn't undone the buttons. "Here." She came to his rescue, going on tiptoe to open the top button and then tugging on the shirt to get it down past his wide shoulders. "You can't even be trusted to dress yourself," she grumbled, but at the same time she let her fingers graze the smooth naked flesh she was covering. She then let her hands rest for a moment at his hips, and when he wrapped her in his arms, she could only sigh and close her eyes, reveling in his warmth.

"I'm back," called Aunt Doris from the living room.

"She's back," Ross whispered into Charity's silky hair.

"Okay." Charity steeled herself, pulling away. "Let's go."

Breakfast went beautifully, even if Charity did have to sneak peeks into a cookbook to find out just how long you really boiled a three-minute egg. "Well, it could have been a trick name," she told Ross when he caught her at it.

"I'm sorry I've inconvenienced you with this change of arrival time," Doris told them both. She was seated at the enormous new table and looking pleased. Charity had found lacy place mats and was using her best china. Orange juice sparkled in the juice tumbler. Charity's silver gleamed beside the plate, resting on a linen napkin. "A friend offered to fly me out in his corporate jet," Doris went on. "And I couldn't pass that up, now could I?"

"Of course not, and we're glad you're here," Charity assured her.

The funny thing was that her words were true. She came out with more coffee, pouring first for Doris and then for Ross. As she sat down herself, Charity looked at the older woman with genuine affection. Aunt Doris never aged. She'd hit fifty-five and was planning to stay there for the rest of her life. Charity had no idea how old she really was, but she thought it had to be somewhere in her late sixties. Yet she looked hearty enough to climb Rattlesnake Trail that morning and take in a few surfing lessons in the afternoon.

"It really is good to see you," Charity said warmly, patting Doris's shoulder.

Doris smiled, then looked about the room, her expression drooping a bit. "I was under the impression that Mason was staying with you," she said.

"Mason is on a... a business trip." Charity bit her tongue, avoiding Ross's glance, knowing she was lying to Doris just the way Mason had, to protect her from the truth. But what could she do? Tell her that Mason had left because he didn't dare face her with his own lies? Charity leaned forward in her chair and took a sip of her coffee.

"Your apartment is lovely," Doris announced as she buttered her toast. "You have such exquisite taste, my dear. I never would have believed it in the old days."

Ross threw Charity a look of pure triumph and, when she was sure Doris's attention was elsewhere, Charity made an insulting face at him. Now the furniture would have to stay until Aunt Doris left.

"And now, Ross." Aunt Doris put down her utensils and wiped her mouth with her napkin. Her benign smile left no doubt that she was coming to the thrust of her visit—the inquisition into Ross's character and fitness as Charity's man.

"You do look like a fine young man," Doris said, though she was frowning as she let her gaze run over him. "But I was surprised that the two of you would go ahead and marry without informing me."

Charity's mouth went dry. This was one of those devastating little details they hadn't cleared up. "I... it was such a spur-of-the-moment thing...."

"And then she didn't know how to tell you," Ross interjected smoothly. "Charity composed letter after letter to you in her head, but she knew there was just no excuse for not having announced our marriage to you ahead of time, so she kept putting off telling you until she could think of a good way of doing it."

"And Mason beat me to the punch," she added. She searched Doris's face, hoping against hope that she would buy the story.

"Well, I know I'm not your mother," Doris said quietly. "You don't really owe me anything—"

"Oh, but I do!" Charity reached out and gave her a heartfelt hug. "I owe you so much, Aunt Doris, and you know it."

Doris patted her hand. "Never mind that, darling. What I'm concerned about is this man you've married. Does he treat you well?"

Charity and Ross exchanged glances. "Of course," she said faintly.

"Is he prepared to provide for you and your children, when you have them?"

"Don't worry about that," Ross said quickly.

Doris turned toward him. "I understand you're a neurologist?" she said complacently.

Charity met Ross's gaze and they both blanched. Seemingly there were a few details of Mason's story that he had neglected to fill in for them.

"That's a rewarding career but a demanding one. Neurology is such a specialized field, it must take up an awful lot of your time," Aunt Doris went on, heedless of the growing tension around her. She smiled encouragingly.

Ross swallowed hard, knowing he had to say something. For a man used to talking his way into one fortune after another, he felt unusually tongue-tied. He had a nightmare vision of Aunt Doris demanding to see some examples of his neurological skills right here on the spot. "Well...uh...I do dabble in neurology now and then," he admitted reluctantly.

Aunt Doris's gray head snapped back at his words. "Dabble?" She looked aghast.

"Yes." Ross leaned back, managing to appear relaxed. Only Charity could read the panic in his eyes. "Well, there is all that suing these days, and now that Charity is pregnant, I've decided to try my hand at the business world. It's more secure, you know. And I find I'm better suited to the wheeling and dealing."

"Pregnant!" both Doris and Charity cried at once.

Ross looked startled, as though he hadn't been aware of what he was saying. "Did I say pregnant?" He looked at Charity. She shook her head wildly, mouthing, *No, no, no!*

"I meant trying to get pregnant, of course," he corrected, looking pleased with himself.

"Oh." Aunt Doris sank back into her chair and began to fan herself with her napkin. "Oh."

Charity rose and picked up a few dishes. She felt breathless. "May I see you in the kitchen?" she asked Ross, smiling sweetly while her dark eyes flashed fire.

"Certainly." He smiled at Doris and followed Charity through the swinging doors.

She whirled on him furiously. "What did you do that for? How could you?"

He shrugged, looking abashed. "I don't know. I lost my head. I just looked at you, and all of a sudden I thought you looked like you should be pregnant."

"Ross!" She felt like throwing plates. "I wanted to get away from lying to her, and all we're doing is creating new fantasies at every turn. I hate this!"

He caught hold of her shoulders. She looked up at him, her dark eyes clouded with her anguish. He started to speak, then stopped himself, shaking his head. A slow smile curled his lips. "You know what?" he said softly. "That was a good breakfast."

She stopped, staring up at him. Suddenly her anger was doused. "Did you really think so?" she asked, surprised.

His smile broadened, and he touched her chin with his thumb. "Yes, I did. And so did Aunt Doris. Didn't you notice? She ate every crumb you put in front of her."

"She did, didn't she?" Charity smiled, thinking how handsome he was. "But, Ross . . ." Her smile faded. "No more lies, okay? We'll have to stick with the big one, but for the rest, try not to embellish."

"Sure." He shrugged casually. "Unless she asks point-blank where the wedding was, I'll try to keep it on the up-and-up."

"Thanks." She sighed. "Now let's take her around and show her the sights."

"Like the happily married couple that we are," he chimed in, then reacted to her glare. "Okay, okay, like the friends that we are." He stuck out his hand. "How about it? We are friends, aren't we?"

She hesitated, then slipped her finely chiseled hand into his enormous one. "Friends," she agreed. And the day seemed brighter already.

The weather couldn't have been better. An offshore breeze carried the haze away, leaving the Santa Barbara skies crystal blue. Ross drove Charity's Fiat with Aunt Doris in the front and Charity scrunched into the miniature back seat. They cruised out along the shore, then turned in and drove through the lovely Spanish-Mediterranean neighborhoods to the mission.

"This one is called the Queen of the Missions," Ross explained as they walked across the patio where eighteenth-century priests once roamed. "Each of the twenty-one California missions was established a day's ride apart along El Camino Real—the Royal Highway."

"Don't you love these old adobe walls?" Charity said as they walked through the gardens, her hands shoved down deep into the pockets of her denim skirt.

"I prefer red brick myself," Aunt Doris sniffed, stepping firmly across the red tiles. "But I suppose they were few and far between around here in those days."

After a tour of the historic downtown buildings and the restored structures of the *presidio*, she began to change her tune.

"I've got to admit," she said grudgingly, coming out of the old *padre*'s quarters and blinking in the bright sunlight. "Those thick ugly walls do keep a place cool in the summertime."

"Hey." Ross gave Charity an exaggerated poke with an elbow. "That's the first step. She's coming around. We'll make a laid-back Californian out of her yet."

"Don't you believe it," Aunt Doris said with vinegary spirit, but a quick smile for Ross. "I've got too much energy for that."

Evidence was abundant. Before the afternoon was over, she ran the two of them ragged. They raced through the botanic gardens, the Orchid Estates and then the natural history museum before heading out to see the giant fig tree at Chapala and Montecito.

"They say this was brought as a tiny plant from Moreton Bay, Australia in 1876," Ross said, shaking his head as he leaned against the tree. Giant gnarled roots covered half a city block. "I don't think I'd ever really appreciated that before." He stretched and grimaced. "Today I feel like I might have swam all the way from Australia myself."

"Getting tired?" Aunt Doris asked brusquely. "Perhaps we ought to find a place to get a spot of tea to buck this young man up," she suggested to Charity.

Charity nodded dully. "Good idea," she said. A strained smile was her attempt to hide the fact that she was as tired as Ross. "There's a lovely little restaurant near here. It overlooks the shoreline."

A fairy godmother with a magic wand might have whisked them there more quickly, but not much. Soon they were sitting in padded wicker chairs and sighing with contentment, tall, cool drinks in hand.

"Now this is what I call sight-seeing," Ross mused. "A comfortable chair, a delicious drink, and an ocean sunset ready to begin before my very eyes."

"Californians," Aunt Doris scoffed, only half joking. "Lazy hot-tub-loving no-accounts."

"Unlike New Englanders," teased Ross. "Who use credit cards only to hold up uneven table legs, would never drive when they could walk, and claim to enjoy an invigorating swim in an ice-laden stream at least once a day— and never let you forget any of it."

"Darn right," Aunt Doris said, just barely holding back her grin. "I may live in the city, but I'm New England through and through."

Charity watched the two of them as they bantered back and forth. Aunt Doris was enjoying Ross. Things were working out so well, Charity was almost tempted to pinch herself to make sure it wasn't all a dream. Ross was wonderful with the older woman. In fact, he was pretty wonderful, period. All day he'd been there, strong and ready to take over when the situation called for it, but never arrogant, never bossy, never the domineering male. The ideal husband. Good Lord, it was true! she realized. He was perfect.

No, she thought as she watched him, the cynicism of her experience coming in to protect her once again. No, there was no such thing as the perfect man. Sooner or later the truth always had to come out. Surely Ross had flaws, and eventually they would surface. Somehow that thought was strangely comforting, if a little sad at the same time.

"I'm off to freshen up," Aunt Doris said, rising from her seat. "Don't change tables while I'm gone."

"We're too tired to do any such thing," Charity chided. "Unlike you. You look like you could keep this pace up all night if you could find someone to join you." She shook a stern finger at her aunt. "Now don't you run off with a doorman."

Aunt Doris chuckled and disappeared into the crowd. Charity turned to find Ross smiling at her. "How'm I doing, boss?" he asked softly.

She nodded slowly, her eyes sparkling. Happiness filled her. "Great. Really great. I can hardly believe we're not really married myself."

His grin was cocksure. It was obvious he was getting his energy back. "I expect to be well paid, you know," he went on, his voice low and suggestive. "By the way, did I mention that I require payment by the day?"

She controlled her smile with difficulty. "I'll send daily checks to your agency."

He raised an accusatory eyebrow and moved closer toward her. "What about my bonus?"

She widened her eyes innocently. "What bonus?"

His hand slipped over hers. "For being such a good...person."

She grinned, tilting her chin. "Goodness is its own reward."

"Like hell it is," he growled, his fingers curling around her palm in a movement that reminded her of the serpent in the Garden of Eden. "I'll take my bonus in installments." He leaned near, just barely brushing her ear with his lips. "The first one will be due tonight," he whispered.

She looked up and her gaze locked with his, suddenly serious, suddenly a bit scary. Why not? she asked herself. She liked him a lot. She was attracted to him as she didn't think she'd ever been attracted to a man before.

Because, a part of her said stubbornly. Just because.

Ross read the shifting emotions in her eyes as clearly as if she'd expressed them aloud. His lips tightened. He'd never been denied a woman he wanted this badly.

But the anger he half expected didn't flare inside him. As he looked at her chiseled profile, her delicately sculpted ear and the tiny strands of wiry hair that escaped from her slick hairstyle, the only thing he felt was an overwhelming tenderness. And that worried him. He would have preferred the comforting familiarity of anger.

"Hello, Ross. I thought that was you."

Ross looked up quickly. It was Gerald Frame, a frequent tennis partner and sometime business associate. A relationship from his "other" life, and a serious threat. At least the man hadn't used his last name.

"Gerald." Ross nodded but didn't smile, hoping the man would take a hint and move on.

No such luck. Gerald planted his feet as though he were settling in for the duration. A handsome man, his blond hair worn a bit too long in back, he had an eye for the ladies, and he cast it now at Charity. "I was just sitting across the room with the Hendersons, and all through dinner I kept saying, 'That's gotta be good old Ross over there. We should ask him to join us.'"

Ross sighed. Gerald was waiting for an invitation to sit down. "So you've finished your dinner, have you?" He tried to sound pleasant, but failed. "Well, it was nice seeing you."

Gerald wasn't much for subtleties. He didn't budge. "We missed you at the country club last night," he went on, glancing again at Charity. He obviously expected to be introduced and wasn't about to leave until he was. "Marlena said you were off on some wild-goose chase that had something to do with—"

The Dos Pueblos Pier consortium. He was about to say it. And once he'd said it, Charity would know. In the fraction of a second between when Ross realized he was about to be unmasked in the worst possible way and when he realized he had to do something to stop it, he thought of a plan.

"Gerald," he said, interrupting the man at exactly the right moment, keeping his head very still and pretending to be trying not to move his lips. At the same time, he gazed furtively across the room toward a bank of ferns that hid the bar from the dining area. "Don't move!"

Gerald froze, though he became slightly bug-eyed. "What is it?" he whispered, staring at Ross.

"She's done it again, hasn't she?" Ross said in a cloak-and-dagger parody of a snarl, sending a piercing glance across the room at the same time.

"Who?" Gerald began to turn to see what Ross was looking at. He always took everyone seriously, so he believed Ross from the start.

"Don't move, you fool!" Ross grabbed the lapel of his suit coat. "Pamela, of course. Your ex-wife. I just saw the guy. I saw his camera. She's hired a detective to tail you again, hasn't she?"

Gerald paled. "Oh, my God!"

"Don't worry old pal." Ross rose and patted his friend's shoulder. "Come on with me. I'll get you out of here, and then I'll cover for you."

"Would you, Ross? I appreciate it." Gerald came along readily enough, forgetting all about Charity, who sat where she was, looking puzzled. Ross threw her an apologetic glance, then led Gerald away. They'd gone halfway to the door of the restaurant before Gerald began to frown. "Wait a minute," he whispered loudly. "I'm not doing anything wrong. I just had dinner with the Hendersons."

"Sure you did," Ross said sympathetically, nudging him toward the door. "But what will that look like when the pictures are developed? Have you thought of that? Angles are everything. Pamela will claim it's an orgy."

Gerald looked worried. "You've got a point there. She always did make a mountain out of a molehill."

"Exactly." Ross propelled him toward the door again. "Now you just take off. I've seen the guy. I'll cut him off and see if I can't expose that film while I'm at it. Okay?"

"Okay." Gerald sounded just a bit uncertain, but he turned to go. "And, hey buddy, you're a real pal, you know what I mean?"

"I know what you mean, Gerald." Ross's smile was more relieved than affectionate. "Just get out of here."

"Right." He disappeared into the gathering gloom of the evening.

Ross's shoulders sagged, and he ran a hand through his thick hair. That had been a close one. All afternoon he'd seen people he knew everywhere they went, but he'd managed to steer Charity clear of them. He'd had to trick Gerald to get rid of him, but he hardly regretted that. Gerald and his ex-wife were always playing games of this sort, almost as if they couldn't bear to live together but couldn't bear to be totally separated, either. So they'd found a common ground to fight over. Besides, Ross thought as he headed to the table, Gerald cheats at tennis.

Charity was waiting for him, a puzzled frown between her brows. "What on earth was that all about?" she asked.

He slid beside her in the booth, and taking her hand, brought it to his lips. "You wouldn't believe me if I told you," he murmured.

She hesitated, not sure she wanted to know. But one thing was certain, this sudden encounter with someone from Ross's life had jolted her back to reality. The look, the style, the *savoir faire*—why hadn't she realized it before? We missed you at the country club, Gerald had said. Yes, Ross was country club all right. He'd only taken this job as a favor to his sister, who ran the temporary agency. He surely belonged in corporate boardrooms and elegant drawing rooms. Her cheeks reddened as she remembered how she'd reminded him about table manners the night before! Ross was country club and prep school and Ivy League colleges, and what was she? South Sea Islands. He'd even said so himself.

A South Sea Islands girl with a fantasy of being married to a country-club blue blood. She sighed and her smile was bittersweet as she met his gaze. He was still kissing her hand. She'd never dreamed she would enjoy that so much. Finally she laughed, shaking her head. "Never mind," she said, relishing the touch of his lips against her fingers, determined to live this lie to the hilt. "I love a man with an air of mystery about him."

His gaze met hers, and the word she'd used—love—seemed to echo between them. "That's me," he said casually, but under his light sport shirt, his heart was hammering. His hand tightened on hers. "Your mystery man."

Aunt Doris came back to the table, and the food arrived. The trout fried in a crushed macadamia-nut batter, salads made of orange sections and julienne *jicama* and wild rice on the side were California cuisine *extraordinaire*.

"Do you like this?" Ross asked Aunt Doris as they tried their entrées.

"It's all right," she said gruffly. "I can eat just about anything. Just as long as you don't try to make me eat any of that green stuff you all eat out here."

"Green stuff?" Charity frowned, and then the light dawned. "You don't mean guacamole?"

"I do mean guacamole," Aunt Doris said placidly, peeling off macadamia nuts with her fork in order to get down to plain old trout. "And I wouldn't touch it with a ten-foot pole."

The food was actually delicious. The atmosphere was divine. As the sun sank on the horizon, a fiery apricot ball descending into a shimmering silver sea, they all three felt comfortably full together. At peace. Happy.

"Tomorrow night I'll take you to my restaurant," Charity promised. "Then you'll see who sets the standard around here."

"Oh, that's right. I'd forgotten that you had a restaurant." Aunt Doris shook her head. "What an idea. You, running your very own restaurant."

Charity stiffened her back. Her work was very much a part of her sense of identity. "That's what I do for a living," she said evenly. "I run a restaurant."

"And quite capably, too, I'm sure." Aunt Doris's smile was as patronizing as her tone. "But now that you've married Ross, of course you'll give all that up."

Charity and Ross exchanged glances, and for just a second she had a twinge of panic. She'd worked so hard to make the restaurant thrive, and she was so proud of it. Was it to be dismissed as a hobby that was good enough for wiling away the time while she was waiting for her real life to begin? Was it only this phony marriage that would please Aunt Doris?

She shrugged those thoughts away. It was just that Aunt Doris hadn't seen the restaurant, hadn't seen how successful she'd become. Once Aunt Doris had been out for a visit, Charity told herself firmly, her views would change.

"I have something for you," Aunt Doris told Charity as the plates were cleared away. "It's yours, really, but you left it when you moved out ten years ago."

Charity waited while Doris fished in her bag, then gasped when her aunt put a gold heart-shaped locket and chain in front of her on the table.

"My locket!" Gingerly she pried it open. Inside were pictures of her mother, young and smiling, and her father, slightly stern. She closed it again quickly.

"May I see it?" Ross was holding out his hand, waiting.

Her fingers curled around the locket. She wanted to hide it away. She held it very tightly for a moment. "Of course," she finally managed to whisper, and she slowly placed the golden trinket in Ross's hand.

He opened the locket and stared at the pictures for a long time. "Your parents?" he asked at last.

She nodded. Something hot and painful was blocking her throat.

He looked up, his dark eyes unreadable. "You look just like your mother, don't you?"

Charity's mouth dropped open. "No!" she cried. Her hand quickly went to her hair to be sure she still had it tied up tightly in a French twist, not flying all over as her mother wore it. "Not at all." Charity glanced at Aunt Doris, but she merely pursed her lips and avoided her niece's eyes.

"I don't look at all like my mother," Charity said again, calming herself deliberately. "That's a very old picture," she added, as though that proved something. She took the locket, snapped it shut and dropped it into her purse. "Now, what shall we have for dessert?" she asked brightly.

They shared an enormous piece of black-bottom pie. Conversation slowly picked up again, and soon it was back to the light chatter it had been most of the afternoon. They laughed a lot on the way home and were still laughing as they came down the hall to Charity's door.

Charity looked from one to the other of her two companions. Things were going unbelievably well. The patina of middle-class respectability was holding up, thanks in large part to Ross and his charm. Aunt Doris had fallen head over heels for him. "And who could blame her?" Charity whispered to herself with a slight smile as she fitted the key into the lock. Aunt Doris was pleased and proud, and that had been Charity's goal all along.

Just before the door opened, Charity thought she heard voices inside her apartment. But that was impossible. There were only two people in the world who had keys to her place, other than she and now Ross. Mason had one, and the other belonged to...

Faith her sister. When the door opened, Charity's worst nightmare came to life. The prime example of Ames nonconformity had arrived for a visit. And as if that weren't enough, she'd brought along a few of her friends.

Six

The facade of normalcy Charity and Ross had constructed hadn't withstood the onslaught of her sister and her friends. The place was unrecognizable. All the beautiful furniture had been shoved to the side of the room, except for the coffee table, which now stood dead center. On top of the finely rubbed finish stood a tabletop hibachi, coals glowing. Rough sticks were stuck in all around, brown things skewered to the tips. It looked like dinner, but one might not want to get more specific. Charity knew her sister wouldn't eat red meat, but she wouldn't put insects past her.

Pillows had been pulled off the couches and placed about the coffee table on the floor. Faith sat on one, her blond hair billowing about her ethereally, her blue dress, made of something light as a spider's web, falling about her in haphazard folds.

On one side of her sat a short, intense-looking young man, on the other, a tiny young woman with gorgeous blue eyes and chopped-off black hair.

"Faith," Charity said ominously, totally unable to muster a smile of greeting. "How did you get in here?"

Her sister looked up dreamily. "I still have my key from my last visit." She held it up with a triumphant smile. "See?"

Ross came up from behind, taking Charity's arm as though to hold her steady. "Remind me to have the locks changed immediately," she said to him through gritted teeth.

He looked from her to the beauty seated on her floor. "I take it this is your sister."

"Yes." She glanced around quickly to see what Aunt Doris was doing, and found she'd sunk onto the cushionless couch, which was now jammed up against the wall. She was looking suddenly old, fanning herself weakly with her hand. Charity felt sick. She knew Doris hadn't seen Faith for at least ten years. Her memories had most likely softened with time. "My sister," she repeated and sighed. "Would you like a glass of water or something?" she asked her aunt anxiously.

"Herbal tea will fix her right up." Faith had a ceramic teapot and poured some quickly into a black enamel cup, rising to take it to Aunt Doris. "Here you are, Doris, dear," she said affectionately. "It's nice to see you again. I dreamed about you last night. You were beckoning for me to follow you into a room full of toasters, but when I got there, you slammed the door in my face." She leaned down to kiss the woman's cheek. "What do you think it means?"

Aunt Doris stared at her, tried to smile, then looked down suspiciously into the tea Faith had handed her.

"What are these little green leaves?" she asked, avoiding the dream analysis.

"Parsley," Faith told her serenely, turning to sit by the table again. "I grew it myself. I grow everything I eat with my own hands. That way I can be sure I'm not polluting my body."

Charity groaned, then remembered Ross. Her gaze swept up to survey his reactions. His face was expressionless, so she couldn't tell exactly how he was taking this. How else could he take it but badly? A wave of hopelessness crashed over her. Faith was a total flake. Her whole family was a bunch of loonies. Whom was she trying to kid here?

Ross was bemused, actually. He'd heard about Faith, knew she was going to be some sort of fading hippie, but now, presented with the real thing, he wasn't sure what to think of her. She was beautiful in an ethereal way, but her eyes were blank, crystal clear and lacking any evidence of rational thought. Too many visits to the moon for this one, he thought cynically.

"Listen, my friends," Faith was saying, smiling benignly. "I want you to meet Doris and Charity. Both were once a part of my single-family unit when I was young. Before I joined the family of mankind and foreverness." She casually waved a hand. "This is Mandi," she said, indicating the young woman with the bobbed hair. "She's searching for her past identity. I hope you'll all be patient with her and help her in her search." She turned to the young man. "And this is W.A."

W.A., the intense man with beady eyes, wore sweatpants and a large white-polyester blouse with huge sleeves. He stood and bowed formally. "How do you do?" he said stiffly, pulling at his hair with a nervous hand, as though he were worried it might not be wild enough. "I've searched your entire place and can't find the piano."

Charity blinked. "I don't have a piano."

He turned toward Faith, stricken. "No piano!"

"He was once Mozart, you know," Faith informed them seriously. "In a former existence. He must have a piano. He's constantly composing."

"Composing!" Charity choked, rolling her eyes heavenward.

Ross tightened his grip on her arm. "Better that than decomposing," he muttered near her ear. "Be thankful for small blessings." He turned to Faith. "I've got an electronic keyboard at—" he stopped himself just before he said the word *home* and substituted quickly "—at my office. I could have it sent over first thing in the morning. Would that help?"

"Enormously." Faith favored Ross with a slow smile, her silvery eyes glinting. "But who are you?"

"I'm..." The words wouldn't come. He looked to Charity for rescue.

"My husband," she said. She said it defiantly, as though she dared Faith or Aunt Doris or anyone else to contradict her. Looking at Ross, she shrugged helplessly. "Ross Parker, meet Faith Ames."

Aunt Doris had finally regained her equilibrium. Setting down the tea she'd barely touched, she rose at this point and began bustling about the room. "Faith, darling, I never! The outlandish getups you parade around in! Well, you always were a strange one." She shook her head, frowning at her niece. "But this ridiculous barbecue. We can't have this." Grabbing two towels she found lying on the table, she took hold of the hibachi by its side handles and started toward the kitchen. Ross stepped forward quickly to help her, but she nodded him away and marched out with the smoking appliance in her own two hands. "We're going to have to cut your hair, Faith dear," she called back cheerfully. "And find you a nice levelheaded tax accountant to marry. That'll fix you up." The swinging doors closed behind her.

Faith looked at Charity. Charity looked at Faith. Suddenly they were both laughing, and Faith held out her arms to embrace her sister. "Mason called me from Mexico City," she told Charity in a loud stage whisper as they hugged. "He was feeling guilty about leaving you all alone. And since we were in the process of being evicted from our house in Tucson, we thought we'd run on over and see if we could help out." She leaned back to look at her sister, then threw a sideways glance at Ross. "Mason told me about the husband business. You know I don't approve of marriage. It's nothing but a form of slavery as far as I'm concerned."

"Then you'll be pleased to know this one won't last long," Charity told her, pulling away and glancing at Ross herself.

He suddenly felt a bit self-conscious with both women eyeing him this way. "The two of you seem remarkably close minded on the subject," he noted. "I think things are working out splendidly so far." If he'd stopped to think, he would have been surprised to find himself an advocate of the married state.

Aunt Doris came out again, the unidentifiable brown objects that had been cooking on the hibachi now residing on paper plates in her hands. "Here you are," she told Faith, plunking the plates down on the table in front of her. "If you must eat this disgusting stuff. I wouldn't touch it with a ten-foot-pole."

"This is delicious," Faith protested, popping a morsel into her mouth. "Really Aunt Doris. Try some. We call them monkey paws, but they're really made out of—"

Aunt Doris held up a hand. "Don't tell me. Please." She leaned close, looking searchingly into Faith's blank eyes. Faith stared back unblinkingly, perfectly willing to be searched. "It's no use, is it?" Aunt Doris said at last, straightening. "I could knock all day, but there's nobody home." She shook her head and turned to leave. "I'm going to bed. Maybe in the morning we can make some sense out of all this."

"There's no hope," Charity moaned, not half an hour later, as she and Ross escaped into her bedroom and shut the door between them and the shards of remaining respectability that lay strewed all about the rest of her apartment. She'd done her duty as hostess, checking to make sure Aunt Doris was comfortable before providing sleeping areas for all the others and distributing bedding all around.

"I sleep in the nude," W.A. had announced as she'd handed out the covers and pillows. His barrel-shaped chest had swelled with pride. "The way nature intended."

"Great," Charity had snapped. "Just keep your nudity wrapped up in this sheet, will you please? Because I don't want to share nature with you. Even if I should wander out for a drink of water at two a.m."

W.A. had frowned, holding the sheet as though it were something odd and not quite clean. "I'll feel straitjacketed," he'd complained.

"He ought to be straitjacketed," she'd muttered to Ross as they'd left the nomads to their own devices. "And held down and tickled with a feather until he agrees to clean up, get a job and stop following my sister around the desert like a lovesick iguana.''

"Oh, Charity." Faith had stuck her head around the corner and smiled beatifically just before they'd made it to the safety of the bedroom. "Just a warning. W.A. does tend to walk in his sleep, and when he does, he generally crashes into things. So if you hear a lot of banging around out here during the night, it's only him." Her smile had broadened. "Good night," she'd said liltingly, then disappeared.

Charity had stared after her, her own hands balled into fists at her sides. "This entire project is doomed," she'd said at last in Cassandra-like tones. "Doomed."

Ross had taken her arm and led her into the bedroom, shutting the door firmly behind them.

"There's no hope," Charity groaned, leaning on his shoulder. "I think I am going to go out of my mind now. It will be better for everyone."

"No, you're not," he said, setting her gently on the corner of her bed and leaning her against the bedpost. She did as he directed, her mind full of her problems, her eyes seeing only the disaster she was certain lay ahead.

"Everything was going so well," she sighed, wrapping one arm around the wooden post and leaning her head against it. "It was beautiful tonight. She loves us together. She loves you."

"Yes, I know." Ross glanced at her with a half smile. He'd never known a woman to be so open about her feelings, good or bad. He was so different. For him, feelings were something one hid in public and dealt with later. Sometimes in his life it had been so bad he wasn't sure he even had any emotions. But feelings seemed to tumble to the surface with Charity, and his own stirred around her as they never had before. The funny thing was, he was enjoying it. Shaking his head, he tugged his shirt up over his head and threw it on the chair, then reached for his belt.

Charity didn't notice what he was doing. Her gaze was far away, going over the evening. "It was perfect," she mused sadly. "She was happy. And then—" her voice took on a note of tragedy. "—Faith! Mason had to call Faith, and Faith had to come running to help me out. Ooooh." Overcome, she fell back among her pillows with a moan.

"Don't worry." The belt landed atop the shirt, and his hands went for the zipper on his slacks. "Everything will turn out all right."

"Don't worry?" she cried, thrashing among the fluffy pillows. "How can I not worry? Did you see her face when she went off to go to sleep? She's all upset. She can't stand that Faith is like she is."

The slacks were now residing on the chair as well. His thumbs slid under the elastic band on his briefs and pulled them down over his muscular hips. For just a moment he stood there holding them in one hand. The mellow lamp-light played upon the sleek warmth of his nakedness. "But isn't that the whole problem?"

"What?" Charity asked, lying flat on the bed, completely unaware that Ross was naked.

"That Faith makes her cringe." He put down the briefs and reached for his pajama bottoms. "You're supposed to balance that. That's what they count on you for."

She frowned at the ceiling, her hands behind her head. "I'm not sure I know just what you mean."

The cotton bottoms slid on easily, and he began to pull together the tie that would hold them up. "Mason can go off and be playboy of the western world and Faith can wander around the desert like a crazy person, because they have you to stay home and be the normal one. The one who redeems them both." The tie was secure, and he came toward the bed. "Isn't that how this family works?"

Her first reaction was to vehemently deny it. But what he'd said touched a nerve and made her think. She turned on her side as he sat next to her on the bed, and then she looked at him.

Her eyes widened as she took in the splendor of the man in pajama bottoms. He was like a Greek statue that had come to life, its cold marble traded in for rounded flesh and hot blood. She backed away across the chenille spread.

"No, you don't," she said warningly. "You just wait a minute! What do you think you're doing?"

His eyebrows arched, all innocence. "Getting ready to go to bed. What do you think?"

She sat up against the headboard, eyes flashing danger, hands clenched into fists. "Not in this bed, you don't."

"I don't see any other beds in this room." He looked sad when she didn't smile. "You wouldn't send me out into the cold when you've got this big huge bed and all these warm covers."

She crossed her arms and thrust out her chin, arming herself against his charm. "There is no way we are sleeping in the same bed together," she said, her voice rising with emotion. "Just absolutely no way."

"Calm down, Charity."

"I'm quite calm."

"No, you're not." Before she knew what was happening, he had hold of her wrist and had turned her around, so that she found herself lying close against him, her back to him, a prisoner in his hold.

She thrashed helplessly, his hold on her effortlessly confining.

"Calm down," he told her, his lips close to her ear. His free hand stroked her hair. "Let's just talk," he said softly, and almost as though compelled to, she stopped struggling.

"You're so full of tension, you feel as though you'll shatter into a thousand pieces any second." His hand relaxed around her wrist, and she didn't try to get away. "Talk to me. Tell me what you're feeling."

She closed her eyes and tried to steady her breathing. It was strange, but she had a sense that he really cared. And he was right. Her stomach was tight as a knot inside her. Things were spinning out of control, and she felt like a bird keeper trying to get birds into a cage once they'd escaped.

"I'm not feeling anything," she muttered. "I'm numb."

His hand was still smoothing her hair. The gentle touch made her sigh, but she hid it.

"Talk," he coaxed. "Tell me about your family. Tell me what Faith was like as a little girl."

Faith as a little girl. Her mouth curved reluctantly into a smile. "When I was very little, I thought that Faith could fly," she said softly, remembering. "I thought I saw her do it once. I must have been dreaming, but it stayed with me like fact. I was practically a teenager before I realized it couldn't possibly be true."

He chuckled, and she turned so that she could look up into his face. Silver lights seemed to shimmer around him. She reached up and touched one in his black hair.

"You know what you said before, about my family using me as sort of their permission to be wacky?" She turned away again. It was easier to talk when she couldn't see those silver lights. "I think there's some truth to what you say." She swallowed, wondering why she wanted to tell him these things. "But you know what? I use them, too. I don't have to be that crazy, because they do it for me. Do you see what I mean?"

It was a moment before he answered. "No," he said at last. "I don't. I think you're rationalizing."

She sighed. "Maybe." She turned so that she was completely facing him on the bed. "But you know, much as I complain about them, I really adore them," she assured him earnestly.

His forefinger drew a line along her cheek. "Even your mother?"

Her heart turned cold. Her first reaction was to snap at him, draw exclusionary lines beyond which he was not allowed to cross. But she stopped herself. Maybe it was time she answered that one honestly. "There are things about my parents that I can't forgive," she said slowly. "I guess I'm not a big enough person. I just can't do it."

His hands went to her hair, and he began searching for pins and pulling them out. She raised a hand, starting to object, but then she let it fall again and said nothing.

"Look," he said as he worked. "I know your parents, were, well, basically crooks. They ran some kind of con game and they got caught at it. They paid their debt to society. Didn't they? If society can forgive them, why can't you?"

She closed her eyes, enjoying the feel of his fingers in her hair as he prodded for hairpins and pulled them free. "It's more than that." She sighed. She was beginning to relax. "It was the way they raised us, the way they used us. They were—I don't know. Maybe they were corrupted by life in the South Seas. That's why I try so hard not to let the Tropics ooze in and take over my life again."

He glanced down at her pretty face, finding that a strange thing to say. "Just what exactly do the Tropics mean to you?"

She made a face. "Sweat. Bugs. And shame."

"Shame?"

She smiled up at him quickly, then looked away again. "I'll bet you don't know what it's like to be ashamed of your parents, ashamed of yourself for being their child."

He considered. "I guess you're right there. I wouldn't say I'm proud of my family, exactly. I've never really thought about it that way. But certainly I've never been ashamed."

She'd never told anyone how it was, and she was going to tell him. Curious how light-headed that made her feel. Excited almost. "It wasn't as though they protected us from the crimes," she said slowly, her voice shaking just a bit. "They used us most of the time. We were part of their schemes." She cleared her throat, then went on. "I remember once when I was about ten years old, on a little island near Samoa, they ran a magic show. My father could do some simple magic tricks, enough to enthrall those poor people. They didn't have television yet and weren't very sophisticated. So my father would make things disappear and my mother would dance around in a skimpy dress. They were good, I guess, because they really could mesmerize an audience. Then Mason and Faith and I would move through the crowd, picking pockets. We did this routine often, going from one island to the next. But one time the locals caught on to what was happening a little too soon, and we all ended up in jail."

Ross felt his chest tighten. Sweet, lovely Charity, her hair spread out around her on the bed—to think of her in jail. It made him want to hit someone. He forced himself to remain quiet and listen.

"They only had one cell in this place, so there we were, little woebegone faces peering through bars. My father had a friend, Barney McGraw, who ran a glass-bottom boat out on the reef. He broke us out in the middle of the night." She shook her head, remembering. "It was classic, just like in an old movie. We actually sawed through the bars and everything. We climbed out the window. Then we took off in his glass-bottom boat and headed for Apia.''

"No one caught you escaping?"

"Not in time to stop us." She smiled bitterly. "I'll never forget my mother, standing there at the back of the boat, her hair flying out around her face, her arms raised high, laughing at the people back on shore as they began to realize we were getting away. She loved it. It was all a big game to her, and she'd won that round."

He stirred beside her. "You didn't love it, did you?"

"No, I didn't love it." Her voice tightened. "I was so ashamed. I hated every minute of it. I was glad when they were convicted and put away on Tonga. We got to go live with Aunt Doris in Boston." She glanced up at him again, just to see if he thought that was terrible. His shadowed gaze didn't tell her anything, and she looked down at his naked chest. "It was so wonderful there. We had clean sheets at night. Marmalade on our toast in the mornings. It was heaven." She paused, then said more emphatically, "That's what Aunt Doris did for me. She gave me a wonderful gift. She taught me how to be normal. She gave me love, security, supervision, a sense that someone really cared. That's why I feel like I have to repay her by living the sort of life she would choose for me. Do you see?"

She turned to look him in the face and this time he nodded, cupping her cheek with his hand. "I see," he said softly.

She settled back, satisfied. "The other two didn't take to it the way I did. Maybe because they were older, because they were more used to the crazy way we'd always lived. I don't know."

They were both quiet for a long moment. A sound came from the living room—a bumping noise. Ross looked at Charity. "The front door?" he asked.

She listened. It came again. She shook her head. "W.A., walking in his sleep," she guessed.

They were silent again, but the room was alive with awareness. Charity could hear Ross breathing. Finally she put her hand against his chest, spreading her fingers and staring at how pale they looked pressed to the darkness of him. She could feel his heartbeat, and it seemed to her it was very fast, urgent, compelling. For the first time she let herself draw in the full sense of him: the width of his shoulders, the smoothness of his skin, the rock-hard muscles of his abdomen, the long strength of his legs. The full shock of his maleness made her gasp, and she looked up quickly to see if he'd noticed.

His eyes were smoky and he was very still, looking down at her as though he were waiting for something.

"What do you want?" she whispered, searching his face.

Words stuck in his throat, which surprised him. You, was the only answer, and on any other night, with any other woman, he certainly would have said it. Isn't it obvious, darling? Can't you tell that I need you? Can't you feel this attraction like I do? Let me make you feel it…and afterward we'll go out for a cappuccino.

He'd said that, or something similar, a hundred times. And that was exactly why he couldn't say it now. He knew in some inarticulate part of himself that this was different. This was a quantum leap away from those superficial affairs. He didn't want to say anything, do anything, to cheapen this. Whatever this was, he wanted to hold on, to treasure it.

Maybe he wouldn't sleep with her after all. Maybe he would prove to her, and to himself, just how special this was by holding back. "Charity," he groaned roughly, burying his face in her hair. "You drive me crazy," he mumbled, breathing in the sweet, fresh scent of her and wishing he could think of something that would convey better what it was he was feeling.

But Charity knew, and she no longer had any ambivalence. A half hour before, she'd been near hysteria thinking of him in her bed while Aunt Doris was down the hall. But now that was forgotten. All that mattered were the turmoil in his voice and finding a way to soothe him. She wanted to give to him whatever she had, whatever would help him.

Reaching out, she ran her hand down his naked back until it reached the cotton pajama bottoms. Hesitating only a moment, she let her fingers slide beneath the belt line until her palm rested firmly on the small of his back, fingertips pressing into flesh.

"Ross," she murmured.

He rose up on his elbow to look at her, his good intentions in mortal combat with his desire. "Charity," he began warningly.

"Love me," she whispered. Her eyes looked huge in the lamplight.

His entire body shuddered. With a groan, he gave in to what had finally become overwhelming—the need to touch her, the need to feel his hardness against her softness, the need to lose himself in her.

His body was hard and felt right as he lay on top of her. When she said, "Yes," it was a long, ecstatic sigh. She gave him her mouth and cradled him with her hips and trembled with the sensations that quivered through her body. Her breasts ached for his touch, and when he began to unbutton her blouse, she helped him. He pushed aside her bra and kissed her, kissing every inch, tugging on the tips, making her whisper, "Oh, Ross!"

She looked up at his dark face, and she knew she loved him. Suddenly and completely, she was in love.

Love hurt. Love was just a step away from agony. Love was losing control. Love was frightening. But love was what she felt for him. It was too late to pretend any different.

Another crash came from the living room, and then voices. Breathing hard, Ross pulled Charity against him and held her still and close. "What the hell is going on out there?" he whispered.

Charity gasped, feeling like a drowning swimmer coming up for air. The room was still spinning. She took a deep breath. "I don't know," she whispered. "It's probably just W.A."

Suddenly the door to their room burst open without so much as a knock. Charity pulled the bedspread up against her chest and glared at her sister, who stood, hair streaming, in the doorway. "Faith!" she cried.

"I'm sorry, Charity," Faith wailed, "but we have to sleep in here with you." Mandi was right behind her, and they were both carrying their bedding.

"What?" They both said it, Charity in anguish, Ross in anger.

Faith let the bedding drop to the middle of the bedroom floor. "Mason is here. He said guilt overcame him and he had to rush back to help you out with Aunt Doris, but I'll bet he just ran out of money." She began to spread her blanket on the floor. "You should have seen the looks he was giving Mandi. I couldn't leave her out there with him. You know what he's like."

"Faith." Ross's voice was rough as sandpaper. "Did it ever occur to you that you might be interrupting?"

Faith glanced up at the two of them on the bed. She looked unsettled for microseconds, as though that hadn't entered her mind until that very moment. Then she lifted her chin and came toward them resolutely. "And a good thing, too," she said firmly. "Have I ever given you my lecture on the importance of chastity in an intemperate world?"

"I've heard it many times," Charity said hastily. She sighed with exasperation, shaking her head. What was the use? They were obviously saddled with roommates for the night, and that was probably for the best. She glanced warningly at Ross. "I promise to give Ross a blow-by-blow account of all your theories on marriage and man-woman relationships if you promise to get down into your bedding and go to sleep. Okay?"

Faith hesitated. "My theories are more persuasive when I give them myself," she reminded them.

"Exactly." Charity hid a smile. "Go to bed, Faith. We'll talk in the morning."

Faith reluctantly did as she suggested, murmuring to Mandi as the two of them settled in for the night, and then turned off the light.

Charity turned to Ross. His arm slid around her. "Sorry," she whispered.

His arm tightened. "Me, too."

She lifted her face and his lips found hers, pressing softly for a moment in a gesture that filled her with emotion. He let her go, and she slipped out of bed and went into the bathroom to prepare for the night. When she got back, dressed in her nightgown, it looked as though everyone else were sound asleep. She slid under the covers, turning away from Ross. It had been an exhausting day. If she was going to get any sleep at all, she was going to have to pretend he wasn't there. In moments she was asleep.

But Ross wasn't. Lying very still, he watched her long into the night. Moonlight played across her face, spinning gold into her hair. She was lovely, and he couldn't get enough of her. And that very fact was beginning to worry him.

When Charity woke up in the morning, the first thing she saw was Ross, leaning on his elbow, watching her. She smiled and lifted her arms to him. When he bent close, she kissed him and sighed.

"Good morning," he said huskily. His voice didn't seem to work quite right, and he attributed it to early morning rustiness.

"Good morning." She snuggled up closer to him, pulling away covers where they got in the way of direct contact. "What a lovely way to wake up."

He traced her smile with his finger. "I agree."

His body was smooth and warm, and she sighed, pressing her cheek to his bare chest. Don't analyze, she told herself. Don't think about next week or even tomorrow. Just live for the moment. Live for what we've got.

"Charity," he was saying softly, his face in her hair. "You smell like a spring meadow." He'd never said things like that to women before. In fact, just a few days before he probably would have laughed at the corniness of that line. Maybe that was what made the difference, because with Charity, it no longer *was* a line.

"You feel like a hot fudge sundae," she said, her eyes half closed.

He stiffened, then chuckled softly. "Gee, thanks."

"Want to know why?" She took his grunt as assent. "Cool and smooth and delicious," she explained, running a hand over his shoulder, "and at the same time—" her hand lingered over his heart and she looked up at him from under her lashes. "—hot and bad for me."

He held her closer, laughing. "I promise I won't give you cavities," he told her, "or make you gain weight."

"Liar," she murmured, raising her lips to his, but at the same moment, a movement in another part of the room caught their attention. Looking down to the foot of the bed, they found a pair of blue eyes staring at them over the brass railing. The ever-silent Mandi.

The blue eyes disappeared. Ross and Charity stared at the blank spot where they'd been.

"I think we're being watched," Charity whispered.

"No," Ross drawled softly, pulling her into his arms. "It's a figment of your imagination." His warm lips began to deliver small kisses to the side of her neck.

"I wish it were," she sighed, closing her eyes and abandoning herself to his touch. "I wish we were all alone."

"Good thing you're not!" Faith's voice came from the foot of the bed, freezing them again. Then she appeared in the flesh, glaring at them. "Lord knows what trouble the two of you would get into if we weren't here to keep an eye on you," she lectured sternly. "Real husbands are bad enough, Charity," she went on as she made her way to the bathroom, her gown trailing behind her. "But pretend husbands are even worse. If you don't watch out, you'll end up with some very unpretend complications."

Charity and Ross looked at each other as she closed the door with a snap.

"What does she mean?" Ross asked innocently.

Charity's mouth turned down at the corners. "I think she's warning against...falling in love," she said, stealing a glance at him and then looking quickly away. "But we already established that we're not falling-in-love types, didn't we?''

Ross was quiet for a little too long, and when she looked up at him again, her eyes were wide with a question. But he grinned quickly. "That's right," he said smoothly, threading his fingers through her hair. "Not to worry. We're complication proof."

Charity tried to smile back, but somehow the fun had gone out of the conversation. "Well," she said, disentangling herself from his embrace. "I guess it's time to get up and get this day going."

He let her go, though his gaze was slightly puzzled. "What's on the agenda?" he asked.

"Oh, I don't know," she answered, bustling about the room, carefully stepping over Mandi. "A quiet morning, I think. A picnic lunch at Stow Grove Park. An afternoon sail and then dinner at my restaurant." She nodded decisively. "Yes, I want Aunt Doris to see what I've done with it." She glanced at him. "And maybe all the rest of you, too."

He hesitated, watching her slip into her fuzzy blue robe. "I've been to your restaurant," he said at last. "It's terrific."

She looked up, her face bright with his praise. "Did you really like it? I'm so glad. I wish..." She shrugged, just a little embarrassed. "I don't know why I didn't notice you. When were you in?"

It had been a Sunday afternoon. He'd chosen it purposely as an empty time when he could take a close look at the decorating and study the ambience. Charity hadn't been in that afternoon, which had suited him fine, as well. He'd been there gearing up for action, not making a friendly call.

He moved restlessly on the bed, wondering if this was the proper time to tell her. What would she do when she found out he was really Ross Carpenter, the hated interloper who she thought wanted to rip her business out of her control? It was time to find out.

"It was a Sunday, about a month ago," he said carefully, watching her reaction. "I was there on business."

She looked surprised, and the words stuck in his throat. This was going to be more difficult than he'd thought. He wanted to reach for her, to reassure her with his body before she took on the full thrust of what he was about to say.

"I've been meaning... I've got to tell you this, Charity." He swallowed. She stared at him. "I'm not really who you think I am. I'm really..." His words were drowned out by a tremendous crash from the living room.

"Oh, my God!" Charity cried, gathering her robe together and leaping for the door.

"I'm really Ross Carpenter," he ended lamely as she disappeared from the room, not hearing him at all. He let out a heavy sigh and swore softly.

"I'm really Alice in Wonderland," said a small voice from the foot of the bed. "I really am."

He looked balefully at Mandi. "No kidding."

She leaned her chin on the edge of the bed and went on earnestly. "I must be. I do get this strange sensation every time I see a rabbit, and I hate falling down holes, and I can just feel long golden hair around my shoulders." She swooshed her head and fluffed her short black hair as though it had suddenly taken on new length.

Ross was caught between cynicism and sympathy. After all, no one wanted to hear who he really was, either. "There's only one problem with that," he told the girl gently. "Alice in Wonderland was a fictional character. She never really existed."

Mandi blinked rapidly. "Does that mean I can't have been her?"

He nodded slowly. "That's what it means."

Her face crumpled. "Oh. Darn."

"Yeah," he grumbled in agreement. "You and me both."

Charity was back. "It was the chandelier," she announced dramatically. "They obviously didn't hang it properly. Someone could have been killed!"

Ross frowned. "It actually fell? All by itself?"

"Yes, it fell." She avoided his gaze. "Not exactly all by itself."

Something told Ross he should go back to bed and not ask for an explanation at all. He gritted his teeth. "Who did it?" he asked.

Charity busied herself gathering bedding together. "Well, W.A. washed out some clothes in the kitchen sink, and he thought he would just hang them somewhere out of the way to dry, and the chandelier seemed like the perfect place...."

Ross groaned. "Say no more," he said, shaking his head. "I'll call a repairman. Just keep W.A. away from open flames and electric sockets. He's lethal."

"Thanks." She smiled and touched his cheek. She'd obviously forgotten all about what he'd been trying to tell her earlier. "I know this is all kind of crazy around here," she began.

"Kind of!" He glanced at Mandi, who was watching them with great interest. "You might say that." But he smiled at Charity and reassured her, "I can handle it."

"Can you?" She wondered. Wouldn't it be wonderful if that were true?

Seven

———

The day went pretty much as Charity had outlined. The repairman Ross called took care of the chandelier, which was remarkably undamaged by its trip to the ground. There was a wrangle at breakfast over who would do the cooking. Charity and Ross won out and spent an hour baking biscuits, frying eggs and broiling crisp bacon that filled the apartment with a cheerful aroma, much to the disgust of Faith and her little group. They opted for nuts and berries that they'd brought along with them.

Altogether, things weren't quite as peaceful as Charity had envisioned. Family discussions went quickly from speculation to heated accusation, with one person after another getting his or her feelings hurt. Faith tried to lecture Aunt Doris on her eating habits, but the older woman would have none of it and turned to Mason, demanding to know how a grown man could justify wandering the earth like a nomad, with no evident intentions of ever settling down or even pursuing a career other than that of ski instructor. Time and again Aunt Doris turned to Ross and Charity as though they somehow redeemed her faith in humanity and were her one haven in the storm.

Reluctantly Charity came to the conclusion that pretending to be married to Ross had been the right thing to do. She hated lying, but she liked to think that this lie had been a white one. She'd been helping someone, not hurting her. The only way to do better was to marry Ross for real.

That thought shook her, and she pushed it away into the margins of her concerns. But every time she looked at him, it grew stronger and stronger.

It was late morning when Ross got a telephone call from Henry Mertz, his business partner. Charity was the one who picked up the receiver.

"Is Ross there?" a deep voice asked. He'd been warned not to use the correct last name.

Here was someone from Ross's real life. It forced her to consider that he did have other things going on besides this make-believe marriage. Her first inclination was to slam down the phone and claim it had been a wrong number. There was no one else in the living room at the moment; she could easily do it. She didn't want to share him, didn't want to risk having something call him back to where he really belonged too soon. But that was childish. She killed the temptation and spoke politely. "Just a moment; I'll get him for you."

"How are negotiations going?" the partner asked as soon as Ross got on the line. Henry wasn't really sure of the details, but he did know who Charity was and that Ross was engaged in a delicate operation aimed at getting her cooperation at last.

"Cordially," Ross answered evasively. He glanced at Charity. She was leaving the room, heading for the bedroom. "But so far unfruitful."

Henry laughed. "What I've got to tell you will put that little venture into the shade," he said. "How would you like a trip to Australia?"

Ross's eyes gleamed. "What exactly do you mean?" he asked evenly, holding back his hope. "Not the WesCo deal?"

"You got it." Henry gave a whoop. "They want you in Sydney by the end of the week to finalize plans. Can you beat that?"

Ross was stunned. It had been a bold gamble to bid on the Australian deal. What WesCo had in mind would dwarf all the other rebuilding projects he'd been in charge of. It would also take years to complete. He hadn't thought he'd have a prayer of getting the contract. "They went for it." He sat down heavily in the handy chair. "Wow," he said.

"You've got to get out there and talk to them right away," Henry said. "They want to clear up the paperwork and organize the financing. They want you to talk to the major backers and soothe a few local fears. There will be media interviews. They said your expertise there was one of the big pluses for our side, as they do anticipate some rather sticky problems P.R.-wise. So pack your bags, boy. Get moving."

Ross was a successful entrepreneur, used to winning out, but this was success on a global scale. The challenge was going to be as exciting as anything he'd ever dreamed of doing. Australia. He took a deep breath, savoring the victory.

"I've already checked flights out of LAX. They can book you on the ten-thirty tonight...."

Henry's words seemed to fade in his ear. Charity had come out of the bedroom. She'd changed into a bright blue jumpsuit that displayed her full figure beautifully. Coming toward him with a smile, she filled his vision, filled his senses.

"No," he said softly into the phone. "I can't go."

The silence of disbelief filled the line.

"You're going to have to go, Henry," he said decisively. Charity reached around him for a pad of paper, and he touched her flushed cheek.

"You're crazy."

"I can't help it." Charity winked and disappeared into the kitchen. He felt a sense of loss the moment she left the room. "I'm in the middle of something here that I...have to follow through on. You'll have to do it."

Henry's voice was harsh. "They're not going to like this. They may pull the bid."

Ross sighed. He knew he was being stupid. He never did foolish things. Human considerations never got in the way of his goals. He wasn't even sure why he was acting so foolishly now. He only knew he had to.

"We'll have to take that chance. Stall them. I'll get out there eventually. It will just take a while."

After a moment of angry silence, Henry spoke. "How long?"

"A couple of weeks. Maybe more."

"You're crazy," he said again.

"Probably so." Ross grinned to himself. "Maybe it's catching," he murmured.

"What?"

"Never mind." Charity had come into the room and was walking toward him. "I'll talk to you later," he said, replacing the receiver despite the outraged squawk that emanated from it. Drawing Charity into his arms, he was full of the coup he'd just pulled off, full of his own prow-ess. He wanted to tell someone how wonderful he was, and it hit him that Charity was the one—the only one—he wanted to tell. And the only one he couldn't tell.

She reached up to him. "Kiss me like a husband," she whispered, eyes sparkling.

He pulled her close and kissed her like a lover, but she didn't complain. Still holding her, his hand touched her hair, which she'd twisted into a sleek style. "Wear it down for me," he murmured.

She smiled but backed away. "No. I can't."

"Why not?"

Would he understand? "Because this is me. The me I want to present to the world."

He frowned, watching her, not really sure what she was saying. "It's not the you I first met," he reminded her.

She smiled quickly and turned away. "I know." She bit her lip. "It's time to rally the troops for our picnic," she said brightly. "I'll go see what's holding everyone up."

He watched her walk away, her step light, her body graceful. This charade had gone on for a ridiculously long time. He was going to tell her tonight.

They picked up fried chicken and took it to Stow Grove Park for their picnic. The filtered light spread dappled patterns on them as they strolled among the redwoods, their feet scuffing redwood shavings along with the fallen brown leaves and small cones. Aunt Doris was enchanted with the mystic feel of the place; so were Faith and her clan.

Mason didn't come because he had business to take care of downtown, and besides, redwoods made him sneeze. That suited Faith just fine. She didn't like the way he was looking at Mandi, and she especially didn't like the way Mandi was blushing every time her eyes met Mason's.

"Perhaps therapy could take care of that libido of yours," she'd snapped at her brother at one point.

Mason had laughed. "Then I would hardly be the sweet, loving brother you care so much for."

Faith's gaze had narrowed. "I can see I'm going to have to explain some of the mysteries of the universe to you," she said. "You need educating. We'll find a quiet time today, and I'll begin work on it."

A look of alarm had crossed his handsome face, and that was when he remembered the appointment he couldn't break.

The afternoon sail had only one casualty, when W.A. fell in and ruined his shirt, but other than that, everything went fine. In the evening, Charity took them all to her restaurant.

Ross watched the transformation begin in the parking lot as they arrived. The Charity he knew so well retreated, and in her place emerged Business Woman. She still looked the same—and yet she looked different. Her lips were set in a thin line, her shoulders were straighter, her eyes had a snap to them, and she walked with a firm tap against the ceramic floor.

"Good evening, Nancy," she said to her assistant as they entered the carpeted lobby. "This is my family. I'd like you to set up the embassy table for them, in the bay-window alcove."

"How do you do?" Nancy was just as professional as Charity. She smiled coolly but with complete hospitality. "I'll take care of that right away." But before she left she had one more matter to bring up. Charity's family wandered off to look at the decor, while Ross stayed by her side.

"The Halcombs just called in a reservation for fifteen," Nancy told Charity as the others left them.

Charity nodded, glancing about the room to judge traffic for the evening. "Give them the closed-off section behind the bar," she said. "They always drink too much."

Nancy laughed, her sleek red hair shimmering in the subtle light of the room. "So the staff has been telling me. By the time the main course arrives, the men in the Halcomb party are trying to pinch the waitress, and the ladies are taking bets on the busboys."

Charity groaned. "They are a rowdy group, all right. And to think they're all corporate accountants!"

"It's all those numbers that do it," Nancy counseled wisely. "Too long at the old adding machine and heads begin to spin."

The two of them smiled, and Nancy left to take care of the arrangements they'd set up. Charity turned to Ross. His grin was affectionate. "I'm impressed," he said. "You certainly do have a handle on this, don't you?"

She nodded, not proud, just sure of herself. "I should hope so."

He touched her chin. "How does a South Sea Islands girl come into this?"

Now she was grinning. "Desire. Pure desire. That and the willingness to work hard."

A waiter appeared with a problem, and she was all business again, handling everything with total aplomb. Ross watched her and marveled and wondered what he was going to do when it was time to walk out of her life.

The dinner went wonderfully. Aunt Doris was impressed and said so often. The praise was nice, but the respect behind it was what mattered. Respect was what Charity had wanted, needed, all her life, and now she was getting it in abundance. She was still glowing when they got home.

"I have ice cream in the freezer," she announced. She felt as though some kind of celebration was in order. "How would you all like some dessert?"

"That would be lovely, dear," Aunt Doris said, and then settled down with the evening paper.

"What kind?" W.A. asked suspiciously.

"Butter brickle."

He frowned and fluffed his hair. "Well, maybe just a little." There was a sickening sound as he cracked all his knuckles. "Meanwhile I'll begin limbering up to do some composing tonight." He raised his nose as though sniffing the air. "It's a night for it, don't you think? Romance is riding on the breeze."

Faith turned on Charity and waved a finger knowingly under her nose. "Wasn't that lovely, what he just said? I told you he was creative."

Charity glanced at W.A., who was looking inordinately pleased with himself. "I never denied he was creative," she said archly, grinning at Faith's frown. "I'd say he's creating himself as we speak. But the question is, do you want ice cream?"

Faith looked petulantly out toward the balcony, where Mason and Mandi were huddled in close conversation. "Not until they come in," she said. "I'll eat with them."

Charity shrugged. "Suit yourself." She turned and headed into the kitchen with Ross close behind.

He'd been waiting for an opportunity to talk to her alone all day. This was the first real moment of privacy they'd had.

"I've got something I want to talk to you about," he said seriously, leaning against the counter as he watched her remove the carton of ice cream from the freezer.

"What is it?" She smiled up at him as she removed the lid.

He grimaced. "I've got a confession to make."

"No kidding?" She put a spoonful of ice cream into her mouth and sighed with ecstasy. "Don't tell me, let me guess," she teased, putting that spoon aside and reaching for a larger one to do the serving with. "You just remembered you have a wife you forgot to tell me about?"

He shook his head, frowning. "No. That's not it."

She pretended to think hard. "You really don't like ice cream," she said, guessing. "In fact, butter brickle gives you hives."

"No." His tone was a bit impatient, but she didn't notice.

"Aha!" She shook her finger at him. "You really didn't like my restaurant as much as you said you did, and now you're trying to find a way to tell me the awful truth. Is that it?"

"You know it's not." He hesitated, and she finally began to realize he was serious. "But that does have something to do with my confession. Your restaurant, I mean."

Charity frowned. "What is it, Ross?" she said sharply. "What's wrong?"

"Nothing's wrong." He'd faced senators and corporate power brokers with less trepidation than he felt here. "It's just that . . . I've been lying to you."

Lying? If there was no hidden wife, she couldn't imagine what he could possibly have been lying about that would make him look so stern. A shock of fear ran through her. Her hands gripped the counter and she stood very still. "What do you mean?"

"Charity—" He reached toward her, but she jerked back stiffly.

"Tell me," she ordered.

He wanted to—if he could only find the words. She deserved to hear it from him, but every time he tried to formulate a way of saying it, it sounded worse.

Then it was too late, because Aunt Doris was bursting into the kitchen waving the evening newspaper. "Guess what, Ross," she stated loudly. "A strange thing has happened. They've got your picture in here by mistake."

Charity saw the expression on Ross's face change. She turned stiffly toward her aunt. "Let me see," she said hoarsely, holding out her hand for the paper.

But Aunt Doris was showing it to Ross. "See? They've got it in a story about some other fellow named Ross. He's just landed some major contract in Australia, and there's this long article about it, with your picture attached. Isn't that odd?"

But Ross wasn't looking at the picture. "Charity," he said again, staring at her. She avoided his gaze, feeling shell-shocked.

"I guess it's because the two of you share the same first name," Aunt Doris babbled on. "His name is Ross Carpenter. But they used your picture."

Charity's throat felt tight but she managed to speak. "Ross Carpenter," she echoed. She took the picture and stared at it. "Isn't that strange?" she repeated mechanically. Dropping the paper onto the counter, she turned to the ice cream. "One scoop or two?" she asked Ross, digging the spoon deep into the creamy substance.

"Charity," he whispered, putting a hand on her arm. "I wanted to tell you."

She shook his hand off, moving quickly so that he couldn't touch her. "Here you go," she said with forced cheer, handing out a plate of ice cream. "Sorry I don't have any whipped cream to put on top."

Aunt Doris frowned, not quite comprehending the new tension in the air. But before she had a chance to make discreet inquiries, the sound of raised voices came from the living room. "Oh, dear," she muttered. "They're at it again. Ross, would you come on out and help me? This sounds like it's going to need muscle power behind the threats."

She hurried out of the kitchen to serve as referee. Ross hesitated. He didn't want to leave Charity now, but he didn't want to ignore Aunt Doris, either. "I'll be right back," he told Charity.

Charity stared after him, then looked back at the picture in the newspaper. Why hadn't she realized the truth? She'd been so willing to go blindly on with this masquerade, never questioning why a man like Ross would have agreed to it in the first place. How could she have been so naive?

His name wasn't Parker at all. He was Ross Carpenter, the man who'd been hounding her for months, trying to get her to join his stupid consortium. She grimaced, remembering when the other business owners on the Dos Pueblos Pier had met and she'd been the only one to dissent from the general consensus to go along with Ross and his plans. They'd said Ross Carpenter always got what he wanted, that she might as well give in at once. She'd said no. She wanted independence, and there was no way he could take that from her without her consent. They'd warned her that he'd find a way.

He'd found a way, all right, a very original way. You had to hand it to the man. He was ready to try anything.

She stared at the melting ice cream. There was a lump rising in her throat. Pulling herself together, she quickly filled the remaining bowls, put the lid on the container and returned it to the freezer. She placed all the bowls on a tray, grabbed up some silverware and carried the lot out to the living room, setting it down on the coffee table.

The place looked like an armed camp. Anger filled the room, but Charity couldn't deal with that right now. She had her own problems.

"If you'll excuse me," she said to the group at large, carefully avoiding Ross's gaze, "I'm not feeling very well. I'd like to lie down for a while." She started for the bedroom.

"Charity, please." Ross began to follow her. She managed to smile, still avoiding his eyes, hoping the others wouldn't notice anything wrong.

"I'd like some time alone, if you don't mind," she said as pleasantly as she could.

She made it into the bedroom, closed the door and leaned against it, her eyes closed. She wouldn't cry. This wasn't, she insisted to herself, a crying matter. It was a joke, really. She ought to be laughing.

She took a deep breath and opened her eyes. She needed time to think, and she knew there wasn't much of that. Someone would come in any moment, just as they always did. She was going to have to think this through very quickly.

Ross sat staring after her, oblivious to the arguments that swirled around him. He felt sick. It was his own fault. She should never have found out this way. He should have gotten to her more quickly with the truth.

How could he expect her to ever trust him again? He wasn't ordinarily a liar, and he didn't ordinarily resort to any means to get what he wanted. But how could she think otherwise?

"Damn!" he muttered harshly.

The others stopped and stared at him, stunned, but he didn't notice. Rising from the couch, he strode toward the bedroom and rapped quietly at the door before entering. "Charity?" There was no answer. He pushed the door open. No lights were on, but he could see where she lay on the bed. Entering the room, he quickly shut the door, leaving the lights off. It would be easier to talk in the dark.

"Charity?" he said softly.

She didn't answer, and he could tell that she was upset. How was he going to explain everything so that she would understand? How was he going to tell her that what had started out as a trick had turned into something very different? He didn't want to lose her.

He walked slowly to the bed and sat gingerly on its edge. "Charity, I know you don't want me here right now, and I don't want to sit here making excuses for what I've done, but this is what I was trying to tell you just before your aunt interrupted. It's what I've been trying to tell you for days."

He waited. She didn't speak, make a sound or even make any movement to show that she'd heard.

"I'll admit that this started out with my trying to get close to you in order to plead my case for a business venture. When I was sitting in my sister's agency and you made that call, asking to hire a husband, I thought that the chance of a lifetime had dropped right into my lap. You'd been holding out on me for so long, not even taking phone calls, and here I finally had a chance to get close to you, to really talk to you, to convince you of how good my ideas were going to be for your restaurant."

He paused, realizing he hadn't done any of that. Funny how quickly priorities could change.

"I never meant for things to go this far," he went on, his voice husky. "I never dreamed I'd get caught up in this crazy charade, get tangled up in your life this way. But once I met you..." He swallowed. He'd never said things like this to a woman before. But then, he'd never felt them, either. "I don't know, Charity, if you can appreciate how different you are from most women in my life. You came at me like a whirlwind and caught me up in your fun, your excitement. I can't really explain it, but I couldn't let it go. I couldn't risk missing a moment of it." His voice deepened with true emotion. All the usual artifices were stripped away, and for once he spoke directly from his heart. "These last few days with you have been some of the best days of my life."

There. He'd said it. And it hadn't really been that difficult.

"Charity? Will you answer me?" He reached out toward where she lay so still on the bed, and his hand found nothing but sheets and blankets. He pulled back, then reached out again. "Charity?" The lump fell apart. There was no Charity lying on the bed. She'd set up a decoy.

"Charity!" He leaped up from the bed, hands balled into fists, and swung around, peering into the darkness. The drapes billowed through the open doorway to the balcony. Three quick strides got him there.

She was sitting on the balcony, her hands folded in her lap. "Charity, damn it," he began, but he stopped when she turned her sad eyes up to stare at him.

"How does it feel to invest all that emotion on a fake?" she asked quietly. "Now maybe you have some idea of how much this hurts."

He sat down in the chair beside her. "I'm sorry," he said simply, swallowing his anger. "I really am."

A man who could say "I'm sorry" was a treasure not to be treated lightly. She smiled in the darkness. "You didn't give your entire speech for nothing," she said softly. "I heard every word."

His hand took hers. "I meant every word."

"Did you?"

His hand tightened on hers. "Are you angry?" he asked.

She was silent for a moment. "Yes," she said at last.

He brought her hand to his lips. "Are you going to push me away?" he asked softly.

Her smile was in her voice. "I don't think I have the strength to do that."

He pulled her into his arms and held her, his face lost in her hair.

"Oh, Ross, Ross, hold me tight," she whispered. "But don't think this is going to make any difference. I'm still not going to join your consortium."

He laughed and her laughter echoed his. Then his mouth was hot on hers, and the laughter evaporated, pushed out by a new emotion that grew like flame on kindling.

But only for a moment. Interruptions were a way of life at Charity's these days, and once again it was Faith who burst in, switching on the light and filling the room with her anger.

"It's happened. I knew it was coming, and now it's happened."

Ross and Charity broke apart reluctantly. "What?" Charity asked, brushing hair from her eyes and blinking in the brightness. Ross's fingers curled around hers, and she clung to his hand, leaning close to him.

Faith looked like a woman on fire. These were clearly tragic circumstances. "Mason," she said, pausing for dramatic effect, "has run off with Mandi."

"What?" Charity looked at Ross. He shrugged.

"It's true." Faith put a hand to her forehead, tragic-heroine-style. "He's taken her. Lock, stock and barrel. They're gone."

"Oh." Charity couldn't work up a whole lot of interest over this turn of events. "That's too bad."

"Too bad? Is that all you can say?" Faith threw herself down on Charity's bed. "She's so young and innocent. I was training her in the ways of a chaste life full of natural fibers and New Age thinking. We'd planned a visit to a trance channeler in Colorado together. She was my protégée. And now she's gone." She pounded little fists into the covers. "How did this happen? How could people like us have such a degenerate for a brother? Where did we go wrong?"

Charity bit her lip and looked at Ross. His grin answered hers. "This has all the makings of a long, long night," he muttered to her. "I think I'll go out and get more ice cream."

She nodded. "Get me a bowl, too," she murmured as he left her. "I'm going to need it for energy." As he closed the bedroom door, she turned to her sister. "Okay, Faith," she said with a sigh, sinking onto the bed beside her, "tell me all about it."

Eight

At breakfast Ross made an announcement. "I'm going to have to go into the office today," he said calmly. "There are some matters I've got to clear up."

Charity looked at him with alarm. "Will you be gone long?"

"Not very." He reached down and kissed her nose. "I'll give you a call from the office and let you know how my day is going."

She tried to smile, but it was hard. Was he really coming back? Was this his way of bowing out gracefully, now that he knew his objective was down the drain?

She was surprised at how easily she'd come to terms with his real identity. After the first shock had worn off, it hardly seemed important. She knew him, knew who he was. The name didn't matter. She loved him, and that was all she knew.

She spent the morning with Aunt Doris, listening to Faith moan about what a snake in the grass Mason was and going through old photo albums, talking.

"Where are pictures of your mother?" Aunt Doris asked at one point.

"I don't have any," she said shortly.

Aunt Doris nodded. "I'll send you some," she replied firmly.

"I don't want any."

"I know how you feel." Aunt Doris frowned at her. "But she's family. She's in our blood, you and me. She belongs to us. We can't deny her. I'll send you pictures," she repeated.

They packed away the photo albums and went on to other subjects. When the phone rang, Charity answered it almost reluctantly. Part of her was sure it was going to be Ross with some excuse as to why he would not be back.

It was Ross all right, but without excuses.

"Charity? I have an errand for you. Go to the dressing table in our bedroom," he said, and her eyes brightened at his designating the bedroom as belonging to both of them. "Get the manila envelope I left there. And bring it to me."

She frowned. This seemed odd. "What are you talking about?"

There was a grin in his voice. "Don't ask any questions. Just do it."

Almost against her will she smiled. She had no idea what he was aiming at, but she knew she wanted to be a part of it. "Shall I come to your office?"

"No!"

"Your apartment?"

"Not on your life. I've got a neighbor who's almost as bad as your family as far as lack of privacy goes. No, I want you to meet me at the Serling Coffee Shop on the corner of State and Balboa. Okay?"

"Okay." She felt like a partner in a conspiracy. "When?"

"Right now. I'll be waiting."

She gave her family an excuse and left, manila envelope in hand. It took ten minutes to drive downtown, and she luckily got a parking spot immediately.

She went inside the coffee shop, but Ross was nowhere in sight. The only people she saw near the desk were a pair of giggling teenagers waiting to be seated, and a man in a fedora, hiding behind a newspaper, like someone in an old detective movie.

She eyed the newspaper for a moment, then stepped closer.

"Psst," came a voice from behind the paper.

"Ross," she said, feeling almost as giggly as the teenagers. "Is that you?"

"Shh." The paper came down to be folded under his arm. There was Ross, his identity hidden under the fedora and behind a pair of the darkest glasses Charity had ever seen. "I'm incognito."

She started to laugh. "What are you talking about?"

"Here." He handed her a pair of sunglasses as dark as his own. "Put them on, fast. We don't want to get caught."

She did as he told her. "Why?" she whispered as he steered her out onto the street and to the corner where he jabbed at the walk button on the light post.

"Just in case."

"In case of what?"

He glanced over his shoulder as two people walked by, then stepped closer and spoke in a confidential tone. "What do you want to bet Faith has followed you? Or W.A.? Or that your brother, Mason, is driving that car right down there by the corner?" He pointed to a pale Mercedes. "I'm not taking any chances. I want one hour alone with you. That's all. But it's something we haven't had since Aunt Doris sailed in the other morning."

"But, Ross—"

"I've booked us a hotel room across the street at the Belvedere."

"Ross!"

"Hey." He turned and touched her cheek. "Don't worry. No pressure." He shrugged, looking young and innocent. "I just want to be alone with you."

She wanted that, too. She shook her head, but she couldn't hold back the smile. "This is crazy," she said as she followed him across the street and toward the plush hotel lobby.

"Isn't that what you're used to? Crazy?" he murmured as they crunched together in the revolving glass door. "I guess it *is* catching. I'll be crazy if I have to." He led her across the lobby toward the elevators.

"But, Ross..."

"Every time I get you alone, someone comes crashing in on us. You just keep those dark glasses on. This time we are going to sneak past them all."

They joined six other people in the elevator, Ross looking suspiciously at every one of them in turn. He nodded for her to get off on the fifth floor, but as soon as the elevator doors closed, he quickly steered her toward the stairs.

"We're actually on the fourth," he told her. "Listen, I'm serious about this. They'll try to find us."

She laughed as she followed him, clattering down the stairs. "What name did you register under?" she wanted to know.

"John Smith. Why not? There are ten other John Smiths registered here, too. It will take them an hour just to go through and check out all the names."

" 'Them'?"

He grinned, steering her down the hall. "The world at large. The evil forces trying to keep us apart."

"Ah." She nodded wisely. "That 'them.'"

Ross unlocked the door and she stepped inside, then caught her breath at the spectacle before her. Pulling off the sunglasses, she gazed about her. The room was full of flowers: spider chrysanthemums, pink carnations, red hibiscus, sprays of baby's breath and a huge stalk of violet vanda orchids in a vase of its own.

"Where did you get these?" She turned slowly to take it all in. Perfumes blended to give the room a tropical feel. She was reminded of the South Seas again, but she ignored the images in her mind. He'd done this for her, and she loved him for it.

"I spent the morning raiding every florist shop in Santa Barbara. I even drove down to Carpinteria to the wholesale greenhouses there."

He picked up a single gardenia, set off by two waxy green leaves. "Put this in your hair," he murmured as he pulled at her pins to let the full weight of her hair fall free.

"Why?" she asked, closing her eyes while he worked, freeing her hair, then attaching the flower with a clip.

"I don't plan to entertain a staid and proper restaurant manager," he murmured, kissing her neck. "I invited you here as a wild island woman."

"Oh. I see! It's just the variety that attracts you."

He put his arms around her and nuzzled her neck. "I have a feeling that you could give me all the variety I would ever need."

She turned to search his blue eyes. Did he sense how much she loved him? "Ross," she began tentatively, thinking she ought to tell him her feelings now, so that there would be no confusion later. She wasn't here to have an afternoon fling. She wasn't here to be part of someone's circus fantasy. Variety was the last thing she was aiming at.

"Hush." He put a finger to her lips. "I said no pressure. Come on over here. I've got champagne on ice."

He settled her into a brocaded love seat and opened the tall, golden bottle in the silver ice bucket, pouring out sparkling liquid into crystal glasses. She watched him, his face boyishly intent on what he was doing, and she melted inside.

"We've got wine," he said as he handed out the champagne, then nodded to acknowledge her, "woman and..." He pulled the drapes wide so that they could look out over the silver-gray ocean. "A magnificent view."

"Lovely," she murmured, laughing at his enthusiasm.

He sat beside her, and then they lifted glasses in a silent toast. The chime of clashing crystal glittered through the air. They each sipped, gazes still entangled.

Ross was nervous. He hadn't been nervous in a situation like this in years. An urge was growing inside him, an impulse to tell her that she was special, that this was different from any other encounter he'd ever had with a woman. But the words wouldn't come, and the more he struggled with them, the more convinced he became that she wouldn't really want to hear something like that. She didn't want to hear about other women in his past. He would just be unburdening himself to cleanse his own conscience. The past had nothing to do with her.

He looked at her again. Her hair was tumbling about her face. The white gardenia gave her a pristine look, tender, vulnerable. Her eyes were dark and mysterious. Her lips looked soft, pink and inviting.

"Charity," he said, his voice shaking. He reached out to put down his glass, not noticing as half the liquid spilled out. Then she was in his arms, her own glass discarded, too. She was like soft, dark velvet, sliding across his skin like a ripple through water. He couldn't talk, couldn't think. All he knew was her smell, her touch, the sound of her.

"Oh, Ross," she groaned, in a plea for reassurance, a demand for fulfillment and a sigh of satisfaction.

He pushed away her clothing like a man starving for sustenance, starting with her blouse and ending with her lacy panty hose. She shivered as he lifted her and carried her to the bed, placing her gently in the middle of the soft blue spread, then leaning back to take in the whole of her. Afternoon sunlight streamed in and caressed her pink-tipped breasts, her rounded hips, her long, satiny legs. His hands shook as he reached out to touch her. Nothing he'd ever done before had grabbed him inside like this. He'd never felt this reverence mixed with such need.

She lifted her arms to beckon him back. His features blurred in the glare of the afternoon light, but she didn't have to see him. His features were indelibly printed on her mind. When he came close her hands went to the buttons of his shirt, eager to find what was beneath.

She pulled his shirt down over his shoulders, her hands hungry for the feel of his smooth skin. "Just love me," she whispered.

Her body had been made for his. She was sure of that now. His hands were made to cup her breasts, his chest was made to rest her face against, his arms were made to hold her close. As she grew more and more frantic to have all of him, he took her, first slow and steady and maddeningly elusive, then hard and driving, searing her with his abandon, branding her with his heat.

Sweet, aching tenderness, a hot, wild dance that sent her spinning with only his hand to guide her, and then a voice, her own, a scream of ecstasy so pure, she felt tears spring into her eyes. It went on and on, and she couldn't breathe, but she didn't want it to stop, didn't want to think. When it finally faded, she was gasping, her eyes wide open with amazement at how fine it had been. She held his shuddering body as he clenched like a fist and then found release himself.

Slowly they regained breath and found a peaceful respite. Ross looked at her, her cheeks flushed, her eyes bright as midnight stars.

"Charity," he said softly, running a hand down her naked form. "I'm afraid you're addictive. The high I get from you is better than anything I've ever felt before. I don't want it to end."

That was exactly the way she'd been feeling, and she smiled a silent agreement. "How long can we stay?" she whispered, half shy to put her feelings into words.

He grinned, his hand beginning his slow tantalization again already. "Until 'they' find us," he told her.

She sighed with pleasure and arched to his touch like a cat. The longer that took, the better. The luckiest day of her life, she decided drowsily, had been when she'd called the temporary employment agency to find herself a husband. Finding Ross was a godsend, even if it had taken a visit from her exasperating family to conjure up this miracle.

Suddenly they were all gone.

Faith and W.A. were the first to decamp. The two of them took a bus to Boulder to meet with a trance channeler who'd found the secret of life and could put anyone at all in touch with it for only a few thousand dollars.

"You're going to pay to find out the secret of life?" Charity had asked, aghast.

"No, silly," Faith had retorted cheerfully. "I'm going to apply for a job with him. I'm great at this stuff."

Charity had been surprised to find herself sorry to see her sister go. But she was even sorrier about Aunt Doris.

"I had a wonderful time," Aunt Doris said as they drove her to the airport for her flight to Boston.

Charity felt the sting of tears. It would be a long time before she saw Aunt Doris again. What a link to her past the woman was. And it had somehow grown stronger with this visit.

"I'll miss you," she said.

"No, you won't," her aunt said firmly. "You'll be much too busy getting to work on having a baby. And once you have it, I'll be back to help take care of it, you just wait and see." She reached over and patted Ross. "You take good care of my girl. Though I know I don't have to remind you of that. Just seeing the two of you together has relieved any fears I might have had." She shook her head. "The way Mason told me about your new husband, Charity, I just wasn't sure."

Charity stared. "What do you mean?"

"Well, he hedged so, and his story kept changing. I was afraid you were living with some man who wasn't good for you. That was why I came out, to see for myself."

"You're not serious." Charity exchanged glances with Ross. "That was the only reason you came out?"

"To be honest, yes. But I'm glad I did. I found out the truth, and I can go back perfectly content. You've made a good marriage, Charity. I'm pleased."

The two of them watched her board her plane. After the huge silver vehicle taxied out across the runway, they turned and walked slowly to the parking lot together. Neither spoke. Suddenly they felt like strangers.

Finally Charity threw Ross a nervous smile. "I guess we're not married anymore, are we?" she said, trying to laugh and not succeeding very well. "We've been married so long, this feels sort of funny."

Ross put an arm around her shoulders, and they walked that way to the car.

"Are you pleased?" he asked at last. "Do you think we were successful?"

She looked out over the sea of cars while she waited for him to unlock the car door. Mixed emotions filled her. "My objective was to make Aunt Doris happy," she said, even though she knew now that that was only half of the truth. She'd also wanted to make herself happy by gaining a little respect from her aunt. It was time she admitted that. "And I think we succeeded in that, don't you?"

He nodded, then helped her into the car. For a pair who'd fulfilled their objectives, they seemed a somber couple, Charity thought as he got in and started up the engine. Where was the celebration? Where was the relief?

"I guess I'd better pack up," he said, once they were back in the apartment. "I ought to get back to my own place." He stood awkwardly, waiting for her to contradict him.

She didn't understand. She looked at him and then away, her heart aching. It certainly felt as though he would like to get out of her apartment and perhaps her life, as well, as soon as possible. Strain had suddenly sprung up between them, and she didn't know what to say. She couldn't even look him in the eye—couldn't bear to be alone with him at all.

"You know what?" she said, beginning to bustle about the apartment, picking up things as she went. "I really should run out to the restaurant. I've neglected it for days, and things tend to fall apart when I do that." She looked up brightly. "You don't mind, do you? I'm just going to run in. I'll be back in an hour or so."

He stood very still. "I guess I won't be here when you get back," he said quietly.

All her hope died and she looked away. "Whatever you think is best," she murmured, taking up her jacket and heading for the door. "See you later."

Ross watched the closing door, then sank slowly, painfully down into the chair that he had rented for Charity's bedroom. That was where he stayed for the next two hours, until he heard her key in the lock.

"Ross?" She could hardly believe her eyes. "You're still here!"

"Do you mind?"

"Mind?" She laughed, and the world, which had seemed dark and gloomy only seconds before, turned bright again. This was all the reassurance she needed right now. He hadn't run for the nearest exit once he had the chance. He was still here. Racing forward, she threw her arms around his neck.

"Hey!" He rocked back, holding her tight, his eyes closed as he took in every bit of her with all his senses.

"I'm glad you're here. I wanted to invite you to a party." She grinned up at him, happy again. "A slumber party. Think you can make it?"

He grinned back, uncertainty vanquished. "I'll clear my schedule," he said. "As long as you promise this time we'll have the bedroom to ourselves."

They were in each other's arms and it was like old times again. Old times of a day ago. Only this time it was even better.

He did move back into his own apartment the next day, but he called her an hour after he'd left. He called her yet again in the evening when she came back from the restaurant, and she didn't feel deserted at all. In fact, she almost felt loved.

Though he'd never said the words, there was something in the way he looked at her, something in the way he treated her, that made her think it was a possibility. After all, he'd taken her crazy family in stride. They hadn't made him cringe, as they did most people. Could this be the one man in the entire world for her? She lived on hope for two weeks, during which she saw him almost every day. Then he asked her to meet his parents.

"My parents are having a big party on Saturday night," he said one afternoon as they came in from a game of tennis. "They'd like you to come."

She put her racquet away carefully, wondering how she could get out of it, knowing she couldn't possibly.

"Can you get away from the restaurant?"

She steeled herself to turn with a smile. "Of course. Nancy can take over for me. But where do they live?" Could he tell she was uneasy?

"In Montecito."

She'd been afraid of that. Montecito was a wealthy suburb of Santa Barbara. "What kind of party is it? What should I wear? How should I act?"

"Be yourself. In fact, let me buy you a dress to wear, all right?"

She was skeptical, but after all, he would know best how she should dress for his parents. "All right."

She regretted that permission as soon as she saw the dress. It came in a box from the most expensive shop in town, but the sarong-style, body-clinging cotton frock in riotous colors was definitely island-inspired.

"I want you to wear this with your hair down and an orchid pinned behind your ear," he said firmly.

"Oh, Ross!" she wailed.

"Come on now. These aren't business people or restaurant people or any people you need to impress with your professional appearance. These are my parents. And I don't want you to be impressive with them. I want you to be yourself." He touched her chin. "I want them to see you the way I see you."

She waited. Just one step further and he could say something sure and complete about how he felt about her. But he pulled back. "Wear it for me," he coaxed instead.

She turned away, disappointed. "Of course I will," she said, but the tone of her voice was hollow.

The days leading up to her visit to the Carpenter home flew by much too quickly, and as the time grew nearer, Charity began to feel queasy.

"If I come down with the flu, I just won't be able to go," she thought with satisfaction. But the upset stomach never developed into anything serious, so she was stuck.

On the night of the party, Ross picked her up early. She'd worked long and hard on her hair, trying to get it tamed without actually pinning it up, but it was no use. She looked South Seas. She felt South Seas. And when Ross came in and she could see on his face that he thought she was the most beautiful thing he'd ever seen, she was perplexed.

"I hope you don't expect me to go barefoot," she snapped, then immediately regretted her tone.

She might have saved herself the anxiety, because he didn't notice her crankiness. "You're stunning," he told her. "You could wear combat boots and carry it off with that dress on. You're out of this world."

Out of this world. That was exactly what she was afraid his parents would think.

"They're going to love you," he insisted.

She wasn't so sure. Things didn't exactly fall into place once they arrived at the overwhelming Romanesque mansion with the sweeping driveway. A servant in white livery opened her door and helped her from the car.

"Oh, my," she said weakly, looking around like a tourist at Versailles. She'd known his family was well-off, but this was in another universe from anything she'd ever known.

"Come on in," Ross said cheerfully, seemingly unaware of how awestruck she was. "I'll find Jarvis."

"Who's Jarvis?" she asked, running to keep up with his long stride.

"The butler. He's worked for my parents since I was a little kid. He'll take care of you while I go find out how the land lies."

They didn't find Jarvis, so Ross brought her to the library for safekeeping. She looked around at the exquisite leather bindings of the books there. The huge globe in the corner might have been left by Jesuit monks centuries before. Portraits hung side by side all around the room, most of them from another age.

"Who are all these people?" she asked, gazing up at the paintings and at the same time holding on to his arm in an unconscious effort to keep him from leaving her alone there.

He looked up and shrugged with unconcern. "Ancestors."

She sneezed. "Look at that," she said as he blessed her. "I guess I'm allergic to ancestors."

"Nonsense," he said, pulling her close to him and dropping a kiss on her nose. "You must have ancestors of your own. Everyone does."

"Not any that I'd care to remember," she said. "I have a feeling that most of my ancestors were nothing but trouble."

He laughed but pulled away. "You stay here," he said. "I'll be back in no time."

She felt very nervous, but she sat down gingerly on the edge of a chair and waited. There wasn't a sound in the big old house, but perhaps that was just because the walls were so thick that none penetrated. Suddenly, the door flew open, and a man in a tuxedo stepped inside.

He stopped short when he saw her, then frowned. "Who are you?" he demanded.

Startled, she echoed, "Who are you?" without answering his question.

"The butler," he said bluntly, and she breathed a sigh of relief. After all, this might have been Ross's father.

"Oh," she answered, then didn't know what else to say. Something told her one didn't make casual conversation with butlers, but she wasn't sure just what one *did* do.

He looked her up and down. "I didn't know they'd hired Hawaiian entertainers for tonight." His brow furled. "But you shouldn't have come in this way. You should have come in through the servants' entrance. Don't you know anything?" He jerked his head in the direction he thought she should be moving. "Come on along with me," he said with weary patience. "I'll take you to where you belong."

Her impulse was to follow him. She felt an outsider. Obviously she looked an outsider. But her rebellious nature surfaced at his imperial tone. What if I were to marry Ross, she thought impishly, and have this guy fired. She raised her chin and replied in what she hoped was a manner that would put him in his place. "I belong right here," she said firmly. "I'm not part of the entertainment. I'm with Mr. Carpenter. Mr. Ross Carpenter."

The man wasn't fazed at all. "Oh." He raised his eyebrow, looking her up and down again. "I see," he said significantly, his disdain obvious. "One of Ross's girls." He shrugged and seemed to be holding his nostrils closed as though something didn't smell very good. "Very well. Stay if you like." And he disappeared around the corner.

His scornful assessment did wonders for her already wobbly self-esteem. She tried to look at herself in the reflection of the windowpane to see if she really looked like a Hawaiian entertainer, but Ross returned before she was sure.

"Here I am," he said as he entered the room, then opened the door wider and ushered in a tall, lovely lady with shiny jet-black hair and a friendly smile. "This is my sister Marlena. Marlena, meet Charity Ames."

"Charity." Marlena came forward eagerly and took her hand. "I'm so glad to meet the woman who has changed my brother's life."

Charity murmured something polite, thrown off guard a bit. Suddenly she realized she'd expected hostility, not this warm welcome. "I...changed his life?" she asked, bewildered.

"Yes, you did," Marlena said firmly. "He's been a dour workaholic for years. Knowing you has brought him back into the real world, put some fun into his life, and I, for one, appreciate it."

Charity looked at Ross. He was grinning as though he agreed with what his sister was saying. Charity began to smile. Maybe this wasn't going to be such a terrifying visit after all.

Ross's parents were just as nice as his sister, though not as enthusiastic. The five of them had drinks and a nice chat before the other guests arrived, and the party was a knockout, with a hired orchestra and dancing on the terrace. Charity had a wonderful time.

It was only later, when she went over the events and conversations of the evening, that she realized the truth. Nice as they'd been to her, his parents didn't think she was right for their son.

Nine

———

Australia seems so far away.''

The airport was crowded. Ross put down his suitcase and turned to put an arm around Charity's shoulders. "Not so far. It's a small world. Hadn't you heard?" Leaning close he began to sing the small world song softly in her ear.

She laughed as she pulled away, but there wasn't much joy in her heart. Ross was going away three long, lonely weeks. He was excited about this trip. She could feel the anticipation flowing through him. He was halfway gone already, his mind disengaged from the time they'd had together and already mulling over what he was going to do once he got to his destination. He was off to new adventures, and back to a life she'd never shared with him. Fear clutched her heart. Would he forget her?

She shook herself to get rid of that kind of thinking. If she didn't watch out, she'd start to cry, and that was the last thing she wanted to do.

"They're calling my flight." He checked his watch. "What do you know, right on time." He pulled her to him for a last goodbye kiss.

She clung to him. She'd sworn she wouldn't make a scene, but when it came down to it, she couldn't help herself. "Ross," she whispered, hiding her face against his chest.

"Hey." He put a finger under her chin and tilted it up so that he could see the moisture sparkling in her eyes. "What's this? I'll only be gone for three weeks."

"Sorry." She tried hard to blink away the tears and pretend nonchalance, but it didn't work. "I'm going to miss you," she choked out.

Dropping his bags, he took her fully into his arms. "I'm going to miss you, too, Char," he murmured, holding her close, his face in her hair. "You don't know how much."

And then he was gone, walking swiftly to the plane. Her tears fell like rain, making her feel like a complete fool.

Back home, she wandered through her apartment, looking at the furniture she'd decided to keep after all, remembering things they'd done together, finding the shirt he'd worn the night before and holding it to her face, reveling in the joy of loving him.

Then the fantasies began. She drifted in a happy daze, thinking about weddings and babies. The problems began to surface when she tried to visualize what the wedding itself would be like. She could see the lovely graceful Carpenters on one side of the church, the unique and undisciplined Ames family on the other. It wasn't a pretty picture.

Two days went by. He hadn't called. All her worst nightmares swam into focus again. He'd forgotten all about her. He realized now that she'd been nothing but an amusing fling. He'd met one of those gorgeous Australian swimmers and couldn't even remember the name of that strange woman he'd pretended to be married to for a few days a month or so ago. It all seemed perfectly possible, even probable. Yet she knew that all it would take to dispel them would be one call on the telephone.

She stared at the phone a lot that afternoon. "Call, Ross!" she ordered, forcing her mind to project to Australia. "Do it now!"

The telephone rang. She jumped a foot in the air, then grabbed the receiver, her heart pounding. "Hello?" she cried.

"Leo's Pizza?" came the reply in a whining adolescent male voice.

Her heart fell. Her number was close to the pizzeria's. She'd had calls for them before. "No. Sorry, you've got the wrong number."

Putting down the phone, she sighed. Why should he call, after all? They hadn't said anything about him calling. Maybe he wouldn't call once during the whole three weeks. Maybe he wouldn't even think to send a post card.

The telephone rang again. Warily, she put it to her ear. "Hello?"

"Leo's Pizza?"

Suppressing her annoyance, she kept her tone cool. "This is not Leo's Pizza. You're dialing the wrong number. It's zero nine, not nine nine."

The adolescent hung up with a click in her ear, without so much as an apology. She replaced the receiver. The next time he called she'd go ahead and take his order, just to be rid of him.

The phone rang again.

Exasperated, she pulled it to her ear and said, "Leo's Pizza here. What would you like? How about a nice large pepperoni with extra cheese?"

The silence on the line only encouraged her.

"No? We've got a special on Leo's Delight. Everything but the kitchen sink and we'll throw that in, too if you can name who won the Academy Award for best Italian accent in a serious drama in 1958."

"Sophia Loren," he guessed, in Ross's voice.

"Ross!" she shrieked, finally noticing the long-distance crackle on the line.

"I'm glad to see you've taken up a hobby to wile away the lonely hours while I'm gone," he went on calmly. "Knitting or racquetball might have been a little more conventional. But then, who ever said you were conventional?"

It was so good to hear his voice. The doubts were swept away in an instant, just as she'd known they would be. He was Ross, her Ross, and the miles melted between them. He wouldn't forget. And neither would she.

Ross was coming home, due in three days. Charity could hardly contain herself. He'd already begun the journey back, although he was stopping off in New Zealand and Tasmania. She was busy planning for his return, imagining him in every room, imagining what the two of them would do together, when his mother called on the telephone.

"I'm sure you are happily anticipating Ross's return, as we all are," she said after the initial greetings. "And that is precisely why I wish to talk to you. As you know, Ross is arriving Saturday afternoon."

"Yes," Charity said. "I'm planning to drive down to Los Angeles and meet him at the airport."

"Oh, no, no, no, impossible my dear. I'm going to need you here."

"What?"

"Ross's cousin Kenneth has arrived on a short visit and we're having a tennis party that afternoon in his honor. He and Ross have always been so close, and he's anxious to meet you. What we'll do is send over a car to pick you up and bring you here. Meanwhile we'll send a private plane down to pick Ross up and bring him in for the party as well. It will save time all around."

Charity didn't like this brilliant idea in the least, but it looked like there was little she could do about it. Ross's mother was in an organizational mood and there didn't seem to be any way to stop her from bulldozing things into the patterns she'd already planned.

Charity worked hard picking out her outfit for the tennis party. She wasn't going to be tricked into going South Seas again. With complete humility, she put herself into the hands of an upscale saleswoman at the most expensive department store in town, following her advice explicitly. The tennis dress was adorable, the shoes top of the line, the little white socks turned down just right. She tied back her hair with a velvet ribbon and practiced looking perky in the mirror for hours the night before the party. Luckily, her legs were good, as well as her tan, and her tennis game was adequate. She felt ready for just about anything, except for the upset stomach she got again. It must be more nerves over seeing Ross's parents, she decided. Everything would be all right once that ordeal was over. But she still got that same sinking feeling when the long white limousine Mrs. Carpenter had sent for her brought her smoothly up the long driveway to the Carpenter mansion.

"Hello, Jarvis," she said at the doorway, holding her head high. "How are you?"

Only the barest flicker of the butler's eyes showed that he wasn't quite sure who she was and why he was supposed to know her. That reassured her. Not a trace of South Seas left.

"Ah, Miss Ames," Jarvis said as he finally realized where he'd seen her before. "Come this way, please. Mrs. Carpenter would like to meet with you in the library."

Ross's mother rose graciously to greet her. Her sharp eyes took in Charity's transformation in a glance. "How nice you look," her lips said, while her gaze was adding, "Nice try, Charity, but it doesn't quite hit the mark, does it?"

"Thank you," Charity said, murmuring something admiring about the way Mrs. Carpenter looked in return.

The older woman offered her a seat and sat back down at the desk. "I just have a few last minute details to clear up before I go out and begin welcoming our guests," she said. "I wanted you to come in here with me so that we would have a chance to get to know each other better. A few moments alone." Her smile was friendly enough, but Charity couldn't shake the feeling that there was something behind her words that didn't quite gibe with what she was saying.

They chatted for a moment about inconsequential things, and then Mrs. Carpenter caught Charity looking at one of the portraits on the wall. The older woman smiled.

"Andrew Bennington Carpenter," she noted. "He was a Supreme Court justice in the last century. Ross's great-great-grandfather."

Charity gulped. A Supreme Court justice. Not bad.

"Would you like to meet the rest of them?" Mrs. Carpenter said, as though they were alive and waiting there on the walls. She rose from the desk, not waiting for an answer, and began to the left of Andrew. "John Maxwell Bennington," she said, pointing out a distinguished-looking gentleman. "President of Tarrington Tech University in the thirties. He's a great-uncle of Ross's." She went on to a roly-poly individual with the ghost of a smile hiding behind the formal pose. "Stanton Carpenter. United States senator."

She went on and on, touring slowly around the room, pointing out one meritorious person after another—and noting aspects of each that Ross had inherited in one way or another.

"He comes from a line of important and capable people," she explained. "Ross will do great things himself, one day. If he gets the right opportunities. And the right help."

The right help. Was she talking about a wife here? Charity's hands had gone cold. She got the picture. It would have been difficult to miss it. All of Ross's ancestors were distinguished people who had done fine things, but they all had remarkable wives to help them along. How remarkable was she? How could she possibly pretend to be worthy of this family?

"And you, my dear," Mrs. Carpenter said as she finished her round. "What about your people? Tell me something about them."

If only she had the nerve to say what she thought. "They're quite interesting, actually. My parents were a pair of lovable, crazy con-artists who went to jail for their crimes. My mother now reads palms in Hawaii. I'm sure the two of you will get along famously."

But this wasn't a contest of quips, or a one-upmanship of relatives. This was a conversation with the mother of the man she loved. She didn't want to shock her, or to make it totally impossible for Ross. So she smiled instead, covering up the dread and anguish she felt, and she was vague and illusive.

"My family is rather unremarkable, I'm afraid. Not a senator or a judge in the bunch."

"Oh?" One elegantly formed eyebrow arched and the word she'd uttered hung in the air, just the way it had been meant to. "I see."

Yes, Charity thought miserably, and so do I. If only Ross were here to help make her forget what an oddly matched couple they were. Funny, but when she was in his arms, all this didn't matter at all.

Someone did appear in the doorway. Mrs. Carpenter looked behind Charity and her face broke into a genuine smile. "Well look who's here. Come on in, darling."

Charity whirled, hoping to see Ross, but instead she found a tall, slender blond man, looking extremely handsome and extremely spoiled.

"Kenny, come on in and meet Charity Ames, Ross's little friend."

"Charity." He took her hand, bringing it to his lips for a Continental kiss, holding her gaze all the while. "I've heard so much about you. But where is the flower behind your ear, the bare feet, the hula skirt? The tales I heard made you sound straight out of a thatched hut." He cocked an eyebrow his aunt's way. "This doesn't look like beachcomber material to me, Auntie."

Mrs. Carpenter's laugh tinkled brittley between them. "Don't exaggerate, Kenny. He is such a tease." She patted his shoulder affectionately. "I'll leave you in his hands. He'll show you around, introduce you to everyone." She pinched his cheek. "I'm off to greet my guests."

She left the room and Kenny turned to grin at Charity, who was feeling definitely overwhelmed. Not only was she not good enough for Ross Carpenter, it seemed she was being thrown to the wolves. Cousin Kenny's sharp blue eyes certainly had a familiar wolflike sparkle. She'd seen the type before—and hadn't cared for it. But she had to remember that this was a cousin who was very close to Ross. She tried to smile.

"Let the games begin," he drawled suggestively. "The question is, which ones appeal to you? Outdoors—" He nodded his head in the direction of the tennis courts where people were already beginning to knock balls around. "Or indoors." His handsome face leered.

Charity had a quick intuition that she was not going to like Kenny, no matter how much Ross did. "Outdoors, please," she said simply. "I just need something to wile away the time until Ross gets here."

"Ah, Ross." He sighed heavily and she wasn't sure if this was some elaborate hoax he was putting on to amuse her, or if he was serious. "So you're true to your lover, are you? How boring."

She didn't deign to answer that, but walked ahead of him outside. The green lawns spread out from the house like long carpets, perfect and impeccable. Beds of flowers glistened with yellows and reds in the sunlight. And the sound of tennis balls being lobbed echoed between the house and the stand of trees on the other side of the courts.

Tables had been set out all around the edge of the lawn. White linen displayed shining silver and glimmering crystal. Potted violets were centered on each table. Charity had never seen anything so lovely before.

Kenny did take her around for introductions. The grounds were crawling with show business personalities and elected officials of local and state government, as well as industry executives and sport figures. The Carpenters seemed to draw a rather rarefied crowd. It was fun at first, to meet people she'd read about in the paper. But she missed Ross. Where was he, anyway? In the meantime, Kenny was a total pain in the neck, leading her here and there, trying to steal a kiss or put an arm around her shoulders. She was forced to get a bit sharp with him a number of times.

Mrs. Carpenter insisted that Kenny and Charity play tennis. "My dears, you must play, Steve and Muffy McInnes are waiting." She drew them toward the courts, then smiled at Charity. "Now, do you play at all?" she asked in a tone that caused Charity to suspect she'd hoped to see her son's girlfriend humiliated. But she was ashamed of the thought the minute it entered her mind and she banished it.

"Oh, just a little," she said. "I've batted a ball around now and then."

"I'm so glad." Was that smile really genuine? "Come along, Steve and Muffy are our club champions, you know. You'll so enjoy playing against them."

The funny thing was that she did enjoy it. She turned out to be even better than she thought she was. Even Kenny was impressed. Wiping his brow after one particularly good save on her part, he muttered, "Go for it, champ. Thank God for athletic women."

They were in the middle of the last set when she spotted Ross's dark hair across the lawn. "Ross," she cried, clutching her racquet and letting a lob bounce right past her.

"Rats," Kenny growled at her. "Watch the ball."

She couldn't walk off and leave things. She had to continue play. Ross hadn't seen her yet, but she hardly took her eyes off him for the rest of the match. He made his way across the grass, stopping to talk to this knot of people, then that. He was finally home. Her love for him misted her eyes and she almost missed another shot.

Finally she was through. She barely shook hands with the ultimately victorious Steve and Muffy before she was racing across the way toward where Ross stood in deep conversation with a man she knew was the mayor of a neighboring town. She hesitated, not sure if she should interrupt, but when he looked up, his face lit with joy at seeing her and he dropped everything, coming toward her for a huge bear hug in front of everyone.

It was all right. He was back. She could breathe again.

But before she'd had a chance to do more than giggle happily in his arms, Mrs. Carpenter was there again, pulling her away.

"Charity dear, there's someone you must meet. She's head of the Women's Auxiliary and my dearest friend."

Charity looked back at Ross as his mother dragged her away. He was looking after her, his brows pulled together in annoyance.

The next hour was spent much the same way. Every time she came anywhere near Ross, Kenny or Mrs. Carpenter had suddenly found something important for her to do instead. And every time she had a free moment, Ross would be entrenched. Their eyes would meet across the crowd. Their spirits would yearn and touch. But it wasn't enough for either one of them—not by a long shot.

Oh Ross, she was saying silently inside. I need you so much.

She went reluctantly with Kenny to the serving table to get some food. "Do you think I could eat with Ross?" she asked plaintively, no longer caring if everyone knew she was beginning to tire of the separation.

"No way," Kenny replied contentedly. "He's talking to the bank president at First Mortgage. He'll need that man's support on a project he's considering. Contacts like that are precisely what parties like this are for. He won't leave his side until he gets a commitment." He jabbed her with an elbow. "Hey, try some of this thin-sliced ham. You'll love it."

"I don't want any thin-sliced ham." She felt like a little girl pouting and stamping her foot, but she was beyond caring. She wanted Ross, and that was all she wanted.

As though he'd read her mind, Ross looked up at that moment, caught her gaze, and nodded. "Excuse me," she heard him say to the bank president. "I've got something important I have to do."

She stood very still and then he was there beside her, his arm slipped through hers, his breath stirring her hair. "Hi there," he whispered. "It's getting harder and harder to find you around here."

"Can't we run away?"

"You bet," he told her, his arm tightening against hers.

"Oh, Ross!" His mother's voice chimed from the patio. "Don't forget! You promised you'd make the toast at sundown. That's a little over an hour away."

Ross swore softly. "I can't cut out on that," he murmured. "So we'll fall back to plan B."

"Plan B?"

He nodded. "See that mulberry tree at the edge of the yard? Meet me there in exactly..." he looked at his watch. "Ten minutes. Don't be late." His smile warmed her as he touched her face with the flat of his hand. "I promise you I'll be there."

The next ten minutes seemed to drag. Kenny talked to her constantly but she hardly heard a word he said. He didn't seem to notice. The time to meet Ross finally came.

"I'm going to have to visit the ladies' room," she told Kenny firmly. "See you later."

"I'll wait right here," he called after her.

"You just do that," she muttered to herself, pretending to go toward the house and doubling back. And she was off, darting around the hedge, past the fountain, and into Ross's arms.

"I can't stand this," she cried.

"I know. Neither can I. We can't leave yet." His kiss seared her lips. "But we can grab fifteen minutes for ourselves," he said urgently.

She didn't have time to answer before he had her racing along behind another hedge along a cinder path, dodging in and out until they came to a catalpa tree.

"This is a hiding place I haven't used since I was a kid," he told her, looking around to see if they'd been spotted yet. "See how those branches seem to form a ladder? Up you go."

"What?"

"Into the tree. Hurry. See how it leans against the rocky cliff? There's a cave just beyond that ledge...."

There was a cave and it took only seconds for the two of them to reach it, first Charity, then Ross right behind her.

Charity looked around. It was just high enough so that they could stand. It was clean. A bed of soft leaves had been piled against one wall by the wind. "What a neat hideout this must have been when you were a kid," she said.

"It's even better now." His hands slid down her sides. "And it's all ours."

She looked up at him, eyes wide. "You don't mean..."

His face came down, his lips touching hers. "I do mean," he breathed into her open mouth. And then he covered her and the kiss deepened, his tongue exploring, testing, coaxing. "What a relief," he whispered against her cheek. "You still taste as good as ever. It wasn't a dream."

Tension slipped away and she sighed happily. "Ross, I missed you so much." She turned toward him, searching for his mouth. "Don't go away and leave me like that again."

He muttered something she couldn't understand because his lips were on hers once more. She opened to him, hungry for everything he could give her. His hands moved across her back and slipped up under the tennis skirt, sending a thrill through her.

She tried to break away. "Ross, you're crazy, we can't—"

"Oh, no?" His voice was a growl that tantalized her senses. "You just watch me, lady. We can."

His hands cupped her bottom, skin to skin, pulling her up against him and into the heat of his own desire, fully evident within the thrust of his hips. Her arms rose to circle his neck and she arched against him, crying out softly as the sensation of his strength shimmered through her.

He put a finger to her lips. "No noise," he warned, half laughing. "That's the one drawback to making love in the middle of a tennis party."

She sighed, not sure she would be able to remember that rule, let alone follow it. There was no way she was going to deny him what he wanted. She wanted it, too. Maybe it was wrong to do it here, so close to the party, so close to his mother. But she didn't care any more. She was his, all his. And she would make love with him wherever he wanted.

His hands were hot where they pressed against her, and she knew they would soon be conjuring up a heat in her that would be impossible to deny. His lovemaking was so special. He made her feel like a treasure he'd found and still wondered at. She wanted to make him feel special too, if only she knew how.

She pulled away slightly, though he kept their hips fused together. She needed room to begin to unbutton his shirt. She wanted to see him, feel his body against hers, and her fingers trembled as she worked, her breath coming faster and faster as his hands moved on her, one hand slipping between her legs to tempt her with soft, stroking caresses that sent electricity sparking through her.

His chest was magnificent, so strong and smooth, the hair so crisp and alive. She pressed her cheek there, closing her eyes. She loved him. Could he feel it? Did he love her?

"Let me see your breasts," he whispered.

One hand left his chest and went to her tennis outfit. It only took one tug at the zipper to make the top fall away, hanging around her shoulders but revealing her full breasts beneath the white lace of her bra. The nipples were already hard and tight and visible beneath the fabric, yearning for his touch.

He groaned, pulling his own hands back up to reach for her, touching each nipple with the palm of his hand, teasing them through the lace, then pulling aside the bra so that he could catch the rosy tips in his mouth, one by one, stroking and tugging until she whimpered, wanting him hard, wanting him now.

"Where?" she murmured urgently, looking around the cave with passion-clouded eyes.

"Here." He lowered her to the leaves, peeling away the remnants of her clothes as he did so. "Just a moment, Char," he whispered as he worked and she writhed impatiently beneath him. Each touch of his hands, each brush of his fingers, seemed to set her on fire. "Only a moment more."

He shucked away his pants before he came to her. She reached for him, gasping with wonder as she always did at how pure and beautiful and smooth he seemed in his nakedness. The power of him frightened her at the same time it excited her. This was hers.

"Oh, Ross," she whispered hoarsely. "I need you so much."

"Wait," he murmured, his hand sliding from her navel down to nestle into the heart of her warm desire. "I want to be sure you're completely ready."

Her hands closed on his hips, fingers hard, commanding. "I'm ready," she insisted fiercely. "Now! Oh, Ross, now!"

He spread her legs and came inside her, moving slow and easy until she urged him to quicken the pace, her breath coming in shallow gasps. He was what she needed to complete her life, her connection to eternity. At the moment of contact, she became whole, woman to his man, and she felt a flowering inside that widened her eyes, made her whisper, "Oh, Ross!" in a way that sent him spinning out of control.

They soared together, clinging tightly to one another for the ride. White heat became fulfillment, and for Charity, the act itself was first and foremost an expression of her love. She spoke to him with her hands, her body, her whispers of incoherent pleasure. And when their bodies were spent, she clung to him and softly kissed every part of him she could reach, so full of her love for him she could barely breathe. Would he tell her he loved her now? She wanted so badly to hear the words.

They lay side by side, and it was only then that Charity began to notice how prickly the leaves were. She laughed softly, staring at the ceiling of the cave.

He rose on his elbow to watch her. "You are the most beautiful thing I've ever seen," he said solemnly, his hand tangled in her hair.

"You can say that even after you've seen all those koala bears?" she asked, smiling back, still missing the words. Did he love her? Did she want to know, just in case the answer was a bad one?

He grinned and showered kisses all over her face. "This was even better than my imagination," he told her. "And believe me, I imagined a lot while I was gone. Right in the middle of board meetings, sometimes." He kissed her.

She laughed softly. Relief filled her. It was going to be all right. She could feel his love even if he wouldn't put it into words. He needed her just like she needed him.

"We'd better go back," she said, stroking his hair. "Your cousin Kenny will be here any minute. He's been following me everywhere today."

His laugh was short and harsh. "Kenny won't come after you while I'm with you," he promised. "I've had to teach Kenny a few lessons before, and I know he isn't looking for remedial work."

She twisted to look at him. "I thought the two of you were so close."

"Kenny is a worthless parasite," he told her. "He's been foisted on me all my life." He kissed her one last time. "Brush him off like an annoying mosquito," he advised. "That's what I usually do."

Charity sat up and began to pull on her clothes again, hurrying but paying careful attention to detail. She was going to have to face all those people again, and if anyone should suspect what they'd been up to, she'd be mortified. But her mind went back to what Ross had said. If his mother was so wrong about Kenny, might she not be wrong about other things that had to do with Ross? It was worth thinking about.

The first few days Ross was back were sheer heaven on earth. He didn't say he loved her. She was still waiting for that. But he did everything a perfect lover could to make her feel loved. Charity was happy.

It was only when she thought about his mother that she felt butterflies and the doubts began to surface. Was his mother right? Would Ross be better off without her?

Of course she knew—or at least suspected—what his mother had been up to with the tennis party, the litany of famous ancestors, and even with Kenny being so attentive. Mrs. Carpenter would just as soon Ross found himself someone else to love and marry. And Mrs. Carpenter was a woman who acted on her druthers.

If only she had first met his parents at the restaurant, or at some other more formal occasion where she could have dressed the part of Ross's girlfriend. Things might have been different. Their first picture of her had been as a South Seas girl, and that picture would stay forever. If only...

But she knew she'd only be postponing the inevitable. Actually, Ross had been right all along to make her meet his parents in a sarong. That was the way she really was. That other persona, the one who ran the restaurant, was the imposter. The barefoot island girl with flowers in her hair was the real Charity Ames, and this South Sea Islands girl didn't fit in with Ross's family at all.

His family knew it. She knew it. The only one who didn't seem to know it was Ross himself. He didn't show any signs of understanding what his parents had seen right away—that she didn't belong out there in the Romanesque mansion.

The trouble was, the more she thought about his mother and all those important ancestors, the more she began to let the doubts and anxieties mix into her relationship with Ross. It was a viper eating away at the heart of her love for him.

"Aren't you ever going to come live here with me?" she asked him abruptly a few days after he got back. She hadn't meant to say the words that way. She'd meant to invite and coax him with smiles and kisses, because she wanted him with her, wanted him in her bed every night. But the words came out wrong and when he looked at her, his face was impassive.

Something was wrong. He could tell that much. She'd been moody all day. Maybe, he thought as he looked at her, he'd been crowding her too much. Maybe she needed more room and this was her way of confronting the issue. If he said yes, he'd like to move in with her, she would have no recourse. But if he said no, she could always make an effort to talk him into it.

"I don't think so," he said carefully. "My place is close to the office and I have all my things there."

He waited, hoping she would laugh and give his reasons the contemptuous shove over a cliff they deserved. But she didn't laugh. Her face got very still and she nodded.

"All right," she said quietly. "If that's what you want."

It wasn't what he wanted at all, but it seemed to be what would satisfy her, and he was glad he'd done things that way so that the truth could come out. The last thing he wanted to do was anything to mess up this relationship. He'd never known a woman like Charity. He didn't want to do anything to risk losing her.

At the same time, however, his mind was on the Australia project. He'd left things up in the air and would have to go back. Ideas and problems filled his thoughts a lot of the time. Sometimes Charity spoke and he didn't even notice. He didn't want to do that, but he had a lot on his mind, and sometimes it just happened.

Charity didn't nag him about the attention problem, but she was beginning to feel very nervous. Why hadn't he wanted to move in with her? She'd assumed that once he came back from Australia, they would be together. But he obviously wanted a dating relationship, something he could take or leave as he chose. That scared her. Especially now.

The slight case of flu that had dogged her hadn't gone away with the passing of the party. In fact, it got worse, and she began to get a clenched feeling, as though her whole body were waiting for something.

Suspicions filled her and finally she went to the doctor. Suspicions were confirmed. She was going to have a baby.

Chaos ruled her emotions. How could this be? They'd been so careful—except for that first day among the flowers in the hotel room.

A baby. Ross's baby. There was joy in that, and yet, this wasn't the time, not now, not without commitment or a future. Not now that the feeling that she didn't belong in Ross's family was so strong.

She conjured up scene after scene on how she was going to tell him and finally decided on a special dinner. She had no idea at all of how he would take the news.

"I've cooked us dinner," she said when he arrived, half proud, half afraid he would laugh.

"I'm going to enjoy it," he said calmly, not making a joke about her cooking. "I'm sure of it."

What a wonderful man. She loved him more each day. "You just sit out here and let me do the work," she said.

"I've got to make a couple of business calls," he answered. "Okay?"

"Sure."

She went into the kitchen and put the finishing touches on the asparagus and baked potatoes, then got the steaks out and ready to broil. But from the sound of it, Ross wasn't finished with his business calls. She went out into the living room to see what he was up to and overheard the tail end of his conversation.

"That's one advantage I've got," she heard him say with a laugh. "I've got absolutely nothing tying me down."

Her heart went cold. He's talking about business, she told herself quickly, but it didn't help.

"Ready to eat?" she asked with a false smile.

"Sure." But he didn't look at her. He was already dialing another number. "Just one more call."

She stood in the doorway but he was talking and had forgotten all about her. Suddenly she felt very small and lonely.

She went back into the kitchen and broiled the steaks, only charring them slightly.

"You're getting good at this cooking stuff," Ross commented teasingly as they sat at the table, under the chandelier. "Are you practicing up in order to make someone a wonderful wife?"

Charity stiffened. It wasn't a joke to her anymore when he bantered this way. "Maybe I am," she said without smiling.

But he only laughed and began to talk about Australia and how wonderful the land was there.

"Ross," she said at last, swallowing hard and trying to be brave. What if he hated this? What if he got angry? Her throat was dry. "I have something I have to tell you. Something important."

He let a large breath out and nodded. "I've got something to tell you, too."

She looked at him. "What?"

He gestured. "You first."

Intuition told her otherwise. "No. You."

He looked her full in the face. "I'm going back to Australia next week."

Charity dropped the fork she'd been using to push food about on her plate. "Oh, Ross! No!"

"Of course I've got to go back," he said shortly. He looked at her beautiful face and wished he could take her along. How was he going to make it through another trip away from her? He needed her. But he couldn't let her know how much. She was such a free spirit. He didn't want to scare her off.

Charity's face was white. "I don't know why anyone would want to go out there again," she snapped, reacting purely out of hurt. "I certainly wouldn't go there on a bet."

That killed that idea cold. He shrugged. "It isn't like this is a vacation, you know," he said defensively. "I'm putting together an operation that will entail an awful lot of follow-through. I need to be there to make sure things get done right."

Unconsciously, she put a hand over her stomach as though to protect the new life she carried there. "How long will you be gone?"

He hesitated, wincing at the thought of how long he was going to be away from her. "About two months, maybe three."

She would be almost five months pregnant by then. "You'll be gone for Thanksgiving," she said softly.

He turned and stared at her as if that thought had never crossed his mind and he couldn't for the life of him understand why it had occurred to her. Thanksgiving. Of all the silly things to bring up now, when he had just told her they would be apart for three months. Was that all she cared about, that the holidays got taken care of?

She tried to explain around the lump in her throat. "We won't be able to have Thanksgiving together."

He looked puzzled for another moment, then decided to make light of it. He tried to grin, shrugging expansively. "We've never had it together before, you know," he reminded her. "It won't be that much of a change."

Fear welled up in her chest. All he ever did was joke. Couldn't he ever be serious? She stared down at her plate and ate automatically. Ross talked about Australia again, about Vegemite and milk bars. She felt colder and colder and wondered why he didn't ask her to go back with him.

Maybe he didn't think she would be able to take off from the restaurant, but that didn't wash. He knew Nancy could take over, and anyway, he should ask even if he knew the answer would be no. At least he would have shown he cared. The months in Australia would be full of challenge and new experiences for him. But for her, staying behind, alone and lonely, they would be hell.

"You said you had something to tell me?" he reminded her.

She shook her head slowly. "No." Her voice was barely a whisper. "No, it was nothing."

She was hurt and angry and her anger grew during the night as she lay still, after he'd left. He didn't want to hear about a baby, that much was certain. He liked having "nothing tying him down." How had she got herself into this mess? He was obviously trying to draw away, and here she was saddled with a fact of life that was meant to pull them together.

She wanted to tell him about the baby, but she knew what would happen if she did. Reluctantly, but with gallantry, he would insist they marry. She clenched her hands into fists as she thought about it. She would never, never use her pregnancy to get a man to marry her.

For a moment she thought about how it would be if she did. She could see his parents' faces. They would put on a polite front, but deep in their eyes she would see the accusation. She imagined their conversations. "It's the classic story. The little tramp found a way to land herself an upper crust husband, didn't she? Well, she's a crafty bit of baggage. But poor, dear Ross. How will he manage with such a little nobody for a wife? He'll never be able to take her to the club. He'll be ashamed to bring her along to family functions. And what on earth will the child turn out to be like?"

The thought of that scene sickened her. Ross must never know.

Still, she was tempted to tell him many times over the next few days. The opportunities cropped up again and again.

"You're a pretty conventional guy," she said one morning as they ate omelets in a Swiss chalet restaurant overlooking the surf. "But I'm not sure how you stand on things like..." She had to catch her breath in the middle of the sentence. Her nerve almost failed her. Surely he would see right through her and know! "Things like marriage and having babies. Just how important are those things to you?"

Ross searched her eyes, trying to read her motives. Here it was again, another bit of quicksand she'd shoved in front of him. Why was she testing him this way all the time lately? They'd been all through this and decided he could live with her craziness if she could stand his normalcy. Was she having second thoughts?

"Marriage isn't that important to me," he told her, though if the truth were known, he had never given the subject a lot of thought. "And babies are beings totally foreign to my experience. I can take them or leave them."

"You don't feel the need of a baby to carry your name and all that sort of thing?"

He took hold of her shoulders. "Charity, I don't want a baby. I only want you. What do I have to do to get through to you?"

She nodded, but her face was white. "That's all I wanted to know," she said.

Ross frowned. He thought he'd answered in a way that wouldn't threaten her, but she didn't look happy. He was beginning to think the old jokes about never being able to understand women had some basis in fact. If he only knew what it was she wanted, he'd do his best to make sure she got it.

In the meantime Charity had decided once again that telling Ross was the worst thing she could do.

And then he left for Australia, and this time her unhappiness was too deep for tears.

She wasn't sure what she was going to do, but she knew she couldn't stay in Santa Barbara waiting for Ross to come back and spare a few minutes for her and the baby. She had to get out. The first thing she did was make arrangements for Nancy to take over at the restaurant for an extended period of time.

Before she could think of what her second thing was going to be, Mason called.

"Hi, Char," he said cheerfully.

"Ah. The prodigal brother." But she was smiling. She always enjoyed hearing from Mason. "Where are you?"

"Mammoth Lakes. I've been here for a few weeks, and I think I'll stay for the winter."

Good old Mason. He never stayed in places like Pico Rivera or West Covina. It was always Aspen or Chile or Mammoth Lakes. "Is Mandi still with you?"

"Mandi?"

"Faith's protégée."

"Oh, her. No. You didn't think I ran off with her, did you?"

"That was the impression we were under."

His laugh was short. "Well, you can lose it. All I did was take the poor girl home. Faith had her so bamboozled with the search for her past identity, she didn't even have her current identity firm yet. She needed to get home to Denver and get herself straight. So I took her."

That made her feel better. She hadn't much liked the thought of her brother seducing the strange girl. "You really ought to let Faith know. She thinks you're Bluebeard and Casanova all rolled into one."

"Faith will survive," he said. "But how about you? How's your gargoyle?"

"My what?"

"Ross. Have you married him yet? For real, I mean."

Charity swallowed hard, forcing her voice to stay light. "What makes you think I'm going to marry him?"

"The way you two looked at each other. The way electricity sizzled every time you passed one another. It looked like a pretty good match to me."

Tears welled up in her eyes and she thanked her lucky stars that this was a telephone conversation so he couldn't see them. "No," she said quickly, trying hard to keep the tremor from her voice. "As a matter of fact, he's in Australia. We won't be seeing each other for a while." She sailed right into her next topic before he had a chance to ask more questions. "I've been thinking. I ought to take a card from your deck and try a change of scenery."

"Oh?" Mason always did know how to read her and he knew she was avoiding the subject of Ross, but she knew he wouldn't come right out and ask for a full explanation. He was much too subtle for that.

"Yes. How are things up there in Mammoth?"

He paused, then answered cautiously. "Great. I've got a job for the winter. Ski instructor."

Suddenly Mammoth seemed like the place to be. Out of the way. Isolated from the busy world Ross inhabited. The thought of snow and a cozy fireplace seemed like paradise. A haven for her and her little one.

"Know of any good restaurants for sale?" she asked impulsively.

Mason hesitated. "As a matter of fact, I do. A friend of mine is looking for a buyer. It's nothing like your place on the pier, but it's cute. The chef's pretty good. It's a Dutch breakfast place with funnel cakes and Belgian waffles. They serve a great brunch."

Charity made a face. It didn't sound like her sort of place at all, but it was worth looking into. "I'll come up over the weekend," she told her brother. "Do you think you could make an appointment for me to have a look?"

Mason didn't sound convinced that she was serious. "Are you sure?" he asked. "Mammoth is a long way from Santa Barbara in more ways than distance."

"That's exactly what I want," she told him decisively. "The restaurant here is running so smoothly, they hardly need me any longer. I'm ready for a new challenge."

She flew up in order to save herself the ten hour drive, rented a car, and was on her brother's doorstep by noon on Saturday.

Mason's condominium was magnificent. "Wow," she said, looking at his view of the mountains, out across the tops of the pine forest.

"You like it?" he said. "Why don't you stay here with me if you decide to give the restaurant a try?"

She threw him a quick smile that only barely hid the trembling of her lips. She knew he was worrying about her and it made her want to blubber. "Won't I cramp your style?" she said with feigned breeziness.

Mason grinned. "I don't have any style these days."

He put an arm around her shoulders and they both stared out at the landscape. He didn't say another word but Charity knew he was ready to help her. He didn't know what was wrong, but he would wait for her to tell him. He was ready to put his own life on hold if it would do her any good. Tears choked up in her throat and she turned and threw her arms around his neck. He held her while she cried, stroking her hair, and when she was exhausted, red-eyed and sore, he settled her down on the couch and went to the kitchen to make her chicken soup, then told her silly jokes until her wide mouth tilted into smiles again.

"We'll see about that restaurant in the morning," he told her. "And if you like it, I'll help you make the necessary arrangements for buying it and making your move." He smiled at her with dark eyes full of love. "Don't worry, Char," he said, rumpling her hair. "You're not alone."

She managed a trembling smile and whispered, "I love you, Mason." It was so easy to say to him. Why was it so hard to say to Ross?

The mail service to Australia was consistent but slow, and Ross was always moving from one place to another. Therefore, it was three weeks before Ross realized Charity had stopped writing to him. He tried to call her right away but her phone was disconnected.

"What is going on?" he demanded of his sister Marlena on an overseas call. "Find out where she is. Go to her restaurant."

Marlena did as she was ordered, calling Ross back the following day.

"They're not talking at the restaurant. The apartment seems to be empty. I just don't know where she's gone."

Ross made arrangements to return immediately but just before his flight left, there was a major disaster on the site. A crane fell apart, killing two workers, and Ross was forced to stay and help conduct an accident investigation.

It was well into December before he made his way back to the States. Henry met him at the airport. They had a quick discussion about the Australian deal and then Henry said, "Guess what. I've got good news. The Golden Tiger restaurant has finally agreed to join the Dos Pueblos Pier consortium."

Ross turned to him, stunned. "What did you say?"

"It's true. The place is under new ownership and they're a much more reasonable bunch...."

"New ownership." Ross swore viciously. "I don't want the Golden Tiger in our consortium," he snapped to his thoroughly baffled partner. "Get me home. I've got calls to make."

Henry backed away. "But we've got that meeting with the board."

"Now," Ross growled, furious. He strode toward the car like a man with a mission, and Henry walked quickly behind.

Ten

Charity and Mason were sitting at the edge of a crystal lake watching the water lap against a lacy edge of early snow when she finally told him that she was pregnant.

"Oh, my God," he said, turning on her almost fiercely. "How did that happen?"

She smiled faintly. "The usual way." She blinked at his disapproving face and went on defensively. "I'm sure you must have run across this problem from time to time with your wild past."

"Never," he said, frowning darkly and not a bit amused. "I'm always *very* careful."

"Well," she said, looking down at her hands in their black leather gloves, "we weren't."

There was a long silence. Finally Mason spoke again. "Are you going to have it?"

Her eyes flashed. "Of course."

He nodded as though he'd known that all along. "And Ross?"

She shivered. "He doesn't know."

They were both silent again. Something jumped in the water of the lake. There was a splash, then ripples. The air smelled fresh.

Mason turned to her again. "Charity, I'm here for you, but you're going to have to tell me what it is you want me to do. Do you want me to go make him marry you?"

"I don't want to marry him."

He shrugged helplessly. "Do you want me to go beat him up?"

"Don't be silly."

His dark eyes had a haunted expression. "Then what can I do for you?"

Her lower lip trembled. "Just love me and be my big brother while I go through this."

He took her hand, but his expression was still troubled. "Are you going to tell him?"

"No." She shook her head firmly. "I don't want him to know."

Mason sighed. "He has a right to know."

"What?" She pulled her hand back.

"He's the father of this baby, just like you're the mother. You can't deny him his fatherhood."

She stared at her brother. "Since when did you become such a moralist?" she snapped.

He grimaced. "I'm not being a moralist, Char. I'm just facing facts. You've got to do what's right."

This from her wandering playboy of a brother. She was stunned, and she didn't want to listen to him. Facing his kind of facts meant making decisions she didn't want to make.

"But don't you see?" she argued. "If he knows, he'll feel he *has* to do something about it." She shuddered. "I don't want him to marry me because he thinks he must."

Mason frowned. "Would you marry him if it weren't for this?"

She felt small and miserable. "He's never asked me," she said simply.

Mason didn't say any more. They went to the condominium, and then she went to work at her new restaurant, the Dutch Kitchen, where she was busy making improvements and keeping her mind off her condition. But Mason obviously thought a lot about their conversation, because a week later he brought it up again.

"I think there's something you haven't considered," he told her one evening over coffee.

"What's that?" she asked, stirring cream into her cup.

"The baby."

She looked up quickly. "What do you mean?"

"The baby has a right to know its father."

She looked away, pain like a knife in her heart. "I know, but—"

"Char." He put a hand on her arm. "I want you to think about this. I know you claim you hate our parents for what they did when we were young. You think their way of life ruined ours, and that living with Aunt Doris was the best thing that ever happened to you."

She nodded, wondering what he was getting at.

He touched her cheek affectionately with his free hand. "I want you to consider this. I don't think, deep down, that you really feel that way. I think your bitterness, your resentment, comes from being sent away to Aunt Doris."

Her eyes widened. "But that doesn't make sense. They had to send us away. They were going to prison."

"I know. But emotions aren't logical." His hand tightened on her arm. "Think about it. Isn't that really why

you're so angry with them? Aren't you really angry because they denied you parents when you most needed
them? Aunt Doris was wonderful to us, it's true. And she
taught us a lot. But she wasn't Mama. She couldn't take
Dad's place. Isn't that right?''

Charity stared at him. She didn't want to admit there
might be some truth in what he said. It would hurt too
much.

''Charity, listen. Don't do the same thing to your baby.
Don't deny this child its father.''

She pulled away from him and rose from the couch. ''I'll
do what I have to do, Mason. Regardless of your half-
baked theories.'' Angry with him and with herself, she left
him sitting in the late-evening gloom.

But late in the night, she couldn't shake the things he'd
said. She lay on her back, running her hand over her
stomach in hopes of feeling the baby move the tiny little
arms and legs it was busy developing, and it came to her
that Mason was right. She loved her parents. How could
they have sent her away like that? Choking tears that had
lain dormant for years came to her now, and she buried her
face in the pillow to muffle her sobs.

In the morning she searched her old purse and found the
locket Aunt Doris had brought her, the one with the pictures of her mother and father. She looked at the pictures
for a long time, then put the chain around her neck so that
the locket hung over her heart.

Her days were pleasantly full. She was up early in order
to get to the restaurant by four. The Dutch Kitchen opened
for business at six. Hours ran until two in the afternoon.
She was back at the condominium by four. Usually she
changed and went out for a long walk through town, or
into the woods. Mason fixed dinner and the two of them

had heart-to-heart talks before she went to bed and started the cycle over again.

She didn't allow herself to think about Ross. She held him safe in a far corner of her heart, but she didn't dare feel anything. It was as though she knew instinctively that once the floodgates were opened, she might be swept away in a wild tangle of emotion that she wouldn't be able to handle.

Her body was changing. Her sense of balance had shifted, and her focus had centered on the child growing inside her. Carefully and systematically she blocked out everything else. Every minute away from work was filled to the brim with plans for the baby.

One December afternoon, she walked through one set of condominiums and wandered into another. An early morning snowfall had blanketed the mountains with a sparkling cover of freshness. Even the air tasted minty. Her cheeks were bright from exercise in the frosty air. Her knee-length parka was buttoned up to her chin with the fur-lined hood fitting snugly over her head.

It was the height of the ski season and there were people everywhere. But as she turned the corner that would take her home, one figure emerged from the crowd, and the way the man moved was alarmingly familiar, despite the split-leather ranch coat he was wearing. She stopped, paralyzed, wanting to run but unable to move.

"Charity."

He came closer. His blue eyes glittered in the bright afternoon light. He was gorgeous, huge and wonderful, and she had to bite back the cry of joy she felt in seeing him. But the joy was mixed with despair, because she knew she had to be strong.

"Ross." Her hand went involuntarily to her parka to make sure it was closed over her rounded evidence of pregnancy. "How are you?" Her voice sounded remarkably unemotional.

"Not so good." He shoved hands deep into the pockets of his fur-lined jacket. His eyes were cold and wary. "I've missed you."

She avoided his eyes. What was there to say? "Have you?" she murmured.

"Why did you run from me, Charity?"

She shook her head. She hadn't worked out what she would say to him, because she'd hoped that he wouldn't come looking for her. What on earth could she say now that he'd found her?

Charity knew she'd have to tell Ross the truth, and she had to be strong about it. If he sensed how weak she was, he would sweep aside everything she said. And once he took her in his arms, she knew she wouldn't be able to resist him.

She lifted her chin and glared at him. "You made a choice, Ross," she said. "You went away to Australia for three months. I couldn't handle that. I don't want a part-time love affair. I need all or nothing, and you were giving me very little. So I moved on to other things."

He stared at her, hardly able to believe this was the same woman he thought he knew so well. There was no warmth in those dark eyes. She was wearing her hair loose, caught up inside the hood of her parka, but there was not a hint of the South Seas flavor he'd loved so much. There was even a different shape to her face, and a different set to her shoulders. She seemed almost a stranger, but that was something he couldn't accept.

"What are you talking about?" he demanded roughly.

She forced herself to remain cold. "We've each gone our own way. Let's not dredge up old memories now. We've got new lives to lead. Let's just go ahead and lead them."

He didn't say a word. His face was blank and he didn't move. She looked into his eyes for as long as she could, then looked off again, desperate to get away from him. "It's no use trying to rekindle a fire that's died," she said lamely. Turning, she walked away, trying very hard not to walk like a pregnant woman.

He didn't call after her and she didn't hear footsteps behind her, but she didn't dare look back. One block, then two. He must be gone by now. She began to breathe more easily. She turned into Mason's complex, glancing back as she did so. Ross was not in sight, but her heart was pounding anyway. It had been traumatic seeing him. She needed a quiet place to recover in. Looking up, she sighed as she surveyed the stairs to Mason's door. Every day those steps were getting rougher to negotiate, and the high altitude didn't help.

She took them one at a time, going slowly, and when she got to the landing, she unbuttoned her parka to reach for the keys she'd stashed in an inner pocket. But before she got them out, she heard footsteps on the stairs behind her.

She whirled to find Ross coming up to the landing, and she pulled the parka closed again quickly.

"What's the matter?" he said sharply, taking her by the shoulders when he reached her. "What's wrong with you?"

She shook her head, staring up at him. "Nothing—"

"Don't lie to me, Charity. I saw how you were going up these stairs. You could hardly make it. What's wrong? Are you sick? Did you hurt yourself?"

His gaze fell to where her hands were white knuckled, holding the parka closed. His eyes narrowed. "Let me see," he demanded.

"No, Ross—"

"Let me see." He pulled away one hand and peeled back the other. The parka fell open. Her condition was obvious.

"Oh, my God," he breathed. "Charity..." He looked into her eyes, then down again. "That's my baby," he said, his tone reverent. He looked up, joy and wonder filling his eyes. "Our baby," he amended. "Why didn't you tell me?"

It hurt to see his happiness. The temptation to take the easy way out, to smile and tell him, yes, this baby is ours, was so strong, she felt herself swaying toward him, ready to lean on his wide shoulders, ready to let him take over. But she couldn't. For his sake, for all their sakes, she couldn't do that.

"Because I didn't want you to know," she said, her voice harsh and grating.

His gaze hardened. "Don't be ridiculous. We'll get married right away."

"No." She shook her head. "We can't do that." She took a deep breath and plunged into her speech. "We're from different worlds, Ross. I tried to be a sane and sober citizen, and for a while I thought I'd succeeded, but you saw right through me. So did your parents. And I realized I didn't want to turn my back on my family and all the craziness they represent. I love them."

"Of course you do."

"I knew you'd want to marry me as soon as you found out about the baby. But Ross..." She forced herself to meet his angry gaze. "You didn't want to marry me before you knew. You went off to Australia without a second thought, not even thinking that I might want to come along." She shook her head slowly. "We're too different, Ross. We can't base a marriage on a baby alone. It wouldn't be fair to any of us."

Ross looked shell-shocked, as though she'd hit him.

"I'm going in now," she said wearily, reaching into her pocket and this time finding her keys. "I'm tired. I need to rest. You go on back to Santa Barbara or Australia or wherever you need to go." She wanted to touch him, to reassure him somehow. He looked wounded. "Don't worry about me, Ross. About us. We'll be fine." She tried to smile. "Goodbye."

He didn't stop her, and she went inside and closed the door. A few minutes later she heard him going down the stairs. Relief filled her, but she still cried.

Work had been her salvation before, and she counted on it now. She went in early the next morning and spent two hours scrubbing down counters and rearranging stock, feeling pleased with herself for being so good at using mindless work to erase her own thought processes. Then everything fell apart. The first customer, Deirdre, her assistant, let in and led to a table was Ross Carpenter.

When she looked up he smiled and saluted her with a little wave. Gone was the dour face of the day before. What she saw in her restaurant was the man who had made her love him months ago, looking thoroughly lovable again. But she couldn't have that. She marched right over to his table.

"What are you doing here?" she demanded.

He was the picture of innocence. "Having breakfast. Isn't that what everyone does here?"

She put coffee down in front of him and pulled out an order pad. "Fine," she said nervously. "But be quick about it. I'm sure you want to get started for home at a decent hour."

He smiled at her again, his eyes sparkling. "I'm not going home."

Her pencil paused above the pad. "You're not?"

"No. I've taken the condominium next door to where you're staying." His grin broadened. "I'm going to keep an eye on you. And my baby."

Charity's shoulders sagged. "Oh, Ross, please don't!"

"Don't you worry." He patted her hand. "I'm going to be unobtrusive. You'll hardly know I'm there. I won't bother you at all."

That statement turned out to be a blatant lie. He bothered her from the first. To begin with, he stayed in the restaurant all morning, sipping coffee, trying various items from the menu and reading from a book he'd brought along.

"A Mother's Guide to Pregnancy Nutrition," he told her, holding it up. "It's great."

"No doubt." She was setting up the table next to his.

"Okay, Charity." He pulled out a pencil of his own and began to write in the margins. "Let's have it. How many cups of milk would you say you drink a day?"

"That is none of your business."

"Green leafy vegetables? And what brand of vitamins are you using?"

She turned on him, glaring. "I don't have to tell you any of this."

He smiled in the face of her anger. "Don't be ridiculous. This is my baby, too. I have a right to know these things."

"Why are you doing this?" she asked plaintively.

"To prove something to you," he said quietly.

She waited, but he didn't say any more. She went back to work but kept turning to look at him from every corner of the restaurant.

Between questions the telephone calls began to come in—calls from Los Angeles, Santa Barbara and even Australia. "Just bring the phone to my table," Ross said non-chalantly. "I'll take it here."

Finally Charity could stand it no longer.

"This is not your office," she reminded him.

"No, this is nicer than my office. That's why I stay." He smiled at her significantly. "The view, in particular, is much, much better."

She flushed and hurried away. Could you love and hate someone at the same time? She could hardly wait for closing time when she could finally throw him out.

The next morning he was back. This time he brought along a book of baby names.

"We'll work on boys' names today," he told her when she stopped by with coffee. "And tomorrow we'll do the girls' names. Okay?"

"I'm ignoring you," she claimed.

"No, you're not," he responded cheerfully. "How about Adrian? Adrian Edward Carpenter."

She paused, intrigued in spite of herself. "What's the Edward for?" she asked.

"Isn't that your father's name?" he said softly.

She stared at him. "How did you know that?"

He merely smiled. "Or how about Matthew?" he went on. "I've always liked that name. My first polo instructor was named Matthew."

"Polo." She rolled her eyes. "Right."

But she was smiling as she walked away. Why was it he could always do that to her?

"What do you think of Ishmael?" he asked a little later as she passed his table, guiding a party of twelve to their seats. "Too literary?"

She threw him a dirty look and went on, but one of her party paused to make a comment, and before long everyone in the restaurant was discussing what she should name her baby.

"Taffy is an adorable name for a baby," one elderly lady lectured her. "The only trouble is, what do you do with it once the boy's hit puberty?"

"Change it to Clint," someone called over from another table, "and buy him a horse."

"Name a child Albert and he's guaranteed to make good grades," a motherly creature told her.

"No, name him Golden," a young man put in. "It's a name to live up to. He's bound to do great things with a name like that."

"I say she's going to be a girl," a stern-looking woman threw in. "And I think Tracy Marie would be nice. That's my name."

The names flew about the room until Charity was dizzy. She escaped into the back room, then picked out her coat to go outside for some fresh air. She needed to think. She didn't know what she was going to do about Ross. Just by being around he was making her happy. And that was much too dangerous.

She'd made up her mind not to let him do the honorable thing. She'd been so sure that if she weakened, it might be lovely for her in the short run, but it would ruin his life in the long run. But with him around, she knew she was going to have trouble sticking to her guns. So what was she going to do?

She stepped out of the restaurant and onto the sidewalk. The morning had been warm, but a frosty wind was blowing in, and she pulled her collar up around her ears.

"Charity!"

She turned and looked back. Ross was calling from the doorway of the restaurant. She didn't want him to come along. Instead of answering, she turned and began to hurry toward the shopping mall across the street. She hadn't taken three steps before her foot came down on a patch of ice and shot out from under her, and before she knew it, she was coming down hard on the sidewalk, and then the world was spinning, and then it all went dark.

"Charity."

The voice came from far away, annoying, like a persistent fly. She frowned and turned her head to avoid it.

"Charity. Can you hear me?"

She opened her eyes a tiny bit. Bright light stung and she closed them again.

She felt a hand on her cheek. "Charity. Can you wake up?"

It was Ross. Her frown transformed itself into a drowsy smile, and warmth washed over her. Ross. "Hold me, Ross," she whispered, part of a lovely, swaying dream. "Hold me."

His arms were around her, and she snuggled against him happily.

"Charity, darling, look at me."

She opened her eyes reluctantly, then blinked and looked around. They were in a hospital. She was in bed, and Ross was sitting beside her. Reality came back with a rush, and she pulled away from him.

"How do you feel? Are you okay?"

"Headache," she said painfully, wincing.

"They said to expect that."

She remembered and her hand immediately went to her stomach. "The baby?" she whispered.

He took her hand and held it. "They're not sure. They're taking tests."

She nodded, closing her eyes again. She wanted to go back to sleep, to block out her fear. But Ross's insistent voice wouldn't let her.

"Charity," he was saying, "you scared the hell out of me. I'm not going to stand for any more of this foolishness. We're getting married as soon as I can get you out of here."

Her eyes flew open. "No..."

"I'm not listening to any more." He spoke gently but with complete conviction. "Obviously I've done things wrong from the beginning. But I'm going to make up for that now. Charity, I'm not going to risk losing you. Not for anything."

"But if I lose the baby..."

A note of desperation came into his voice. "Don't you get it yet? What do I have to do to convince you?" His hand tightened on hers. "I didn't tell you right, did I? I guess I never really told you at all. But I thought you knew. I thought you'd have to know."

She was struggling to understand. "Know what?"

His eyes were crystal blue, clear and honest. "That I love you."

She lay very still, wondering if she'd heard him right.

"Just tell me one thing, Charity," he went on when she didn't respond. "Do you love me?"

His eyes were open, vulnerable. She could make him or destroy him with just one word. She stared in wonder. "Ross," she whispered at last. "I love you more than life itself."

He made a sound, a strangling sound, and then tears welled up in his eyes. "Charity," he muttered huskily. "Oh, Charity."

He held her and she closed her eyes. "From the first day you walked into my life," she whispered, almost more to herself than to him.

Ross sighed. "Then you'll marry me?"

She shook her head. "No."

He reared back, glaring at her in astonishment. "Why not?"

She tried to smile through her tears. "Because I love you."

"That doesn't make any sense," he growled, his anger barely leashed.

"I know. But it has to be." She shrugged. "Can't you see? You were born into a great family, a family full of important people doing important things. My whole family is ridiculous. I can't conform to all the rules of how people are supposed to behave. I don't fit in with great families. I would only make you miserable."

Ross stared at her as though she were a being from another planet. "What a load of nonsense," he said at last. "Where did you get these crazy ideas?"

She shook her head wearily. "You've got senators and Supreme Court justices in your family," she began.

"Sure I do," he interrupted. "From three and four generations ago. You don't see too many of them these days." He touched her hair. "I'm a businessman, Charity, not a lawyer. I'm not bucking for greatness. My father hasn't done a lick of work in twenty years. He's a fun guy, but he hasn't done much that's 'great.' In fact, it's money I've made lately that's keeping the old mansion afloat."

She blinked at him. "But your mother—"

"My mother is full of dreams, Charity. Not reality." His hungry gaze swept over her face. "I've searched all my life for a woman I could live with. I didn't realize that was what I was doing. But I know now." He bent forward and kissed her. "And you're the one, darling," he breathed against her lips. "It's you or no one."

"But, Ross..." Could it be true? She hardly dared to put her doubts away just yet.

"We're getting married," he said decisively. He took up her hand again and began to kiss her fingers, one by one. Whenever he looked at her, his eyes were full of love. "And if you've got any more objections," he said fiercely, "give them to me now, so I can shoot them down, just like I did that one."

She laughed. She couldn't help it. He made her laugh, and that was one of the things she loved about him. It was beginning to dawn on her that this was working up to a happy ending, and that was something she hadn't expected. "There is our work," she reminded him. "How can we get married when our work will drive us apart?"

"I've got it all figured out. Henry can handle most of the Australia work. I'll have to go for week-long trips maybe four times a year, and you'll take a leave from the restaurant and go with me. How's that? Most of my work is done by telephone, and as far as I know, Mammoth has plenty of those. Plus an airport for quick trips out of town when absolutely necessary."

"Do you really think it could work?" she asked him.

"Of course. But we won't go anywhere until after the baby is born." He looked at her questioningly. "How about it?"

Her gaze held his, her eyes laughing. Slowly she nodded.

"Is that a yes?" he demanded.

She nodded again, and he took her in his arms with a whoop. They clung together, half laughing, half crying, holding tightly until Mason came into the room looking pleased, and they pulled apart to hear what he had to say.

"The doctors wanted me to tell you the good news. You're fine," he told Charity. "A few bruises and sprains, and we're to watch you for reaction to the concussion, but that's all."

"The baby?"

"It's fine." He looked at Ross. "They want to keep her for the night for observation. They'll come in to talk to her, and then we can take her home in the morning."

Ross raised an eyebrow. "Well, Mason, you're going to have to choose whether you want to be best man or give away the bride. Or do you suppose you could do both?"

Mason looked perplexed, and then his face broke into a delighted grin. "Are you two finally getting married?" he scoffed teasingly. "It's about time. I'm sick of worrying about you. Now maybe I can go back to my normal life."

"Anything to make things easier for you," Ross teased right back. "But we'll be living right next door." He turned to Charity and gestured toward her brother. "We've practically got a live-in baby-sitter already."

"Oh, no you don't." Mason started toward the door. "I draw the line at changing diapers."

"We'll be taking this baby everywhere we go," Charity reassured him. "And, Ross, one more thing. When we make that first trip to Australia, do you think we could stop off in Hawaii? I . . . I want my mother to meet you."

Ross and Mason exchanged glances. "Of course," Ross said, waving to Mason as he left the room. "But right now we need to get back to thinking about names." He put his hand on the protruding roundness that signaled their baby's growth.

"Ross if it's a boy," she said weakly.

"Charity if it's a girl," he added.

She shook her head, making a face. "No, one Charity is enough."

He grinned. "Then how about Hope? To round out the set."

She caught his smile and held it. "As in Faith, Hope and Charity?" She lay back, warmth flooding her. More evidence of just how easily he could accept her crazy family. How could she ever have doubted it? "I love you, Ross."

"Just you wait, Charity," he said with emotion filling his eyes. "As far as we're concerned, the loving has only just begun."

*   *   *   *   *

ATTRACTIVE, SPACE SAVING BOOK RACK

Display your most prized novels on this handsome and sturdy book rack. The hand-rubbed walnut finish will blend into your library decor with quiet elegance, providing a practical organizer for your favorite hard-or soft-covered books.

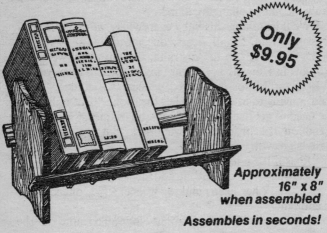

Only $9.95

Approximately 16" x 8" when assembled

Assembles in seconds!

To order, rush your name, address and zip code, along with a check or money order for $10.70* ($9.95 plus 75¢ postage and handling) payable to *Silhouette Books.*

Silhouette Books
Book Rack Offer
901 Fuhrmann Blvd.
P.O. Box 1396
Buffalo, NY 14269-1396

Offer not available in Canada.

BKR-2A

*New York and Iowa residents add appropriate sales tax.

 *Silhouette Desire*

COMING
NEXT MONTH

#439 THE CASTLE KEEP—Jennifer Greene
Although architect Micheal Fitzgerald had made a career out of building walls, he'd never seen defenses like Carra O'Neill's—defenses he planned on breaking down with a little Irish magic.

#440 OUT OF THE COLD—Robin Elliott
When Joshua Quinn was sent to protect Kristin Duquesne, he wasn't supposed to fall in love with her. But he had . . . and now both their lives were in danger.

#441 RELUCTANT PARTNERS—Judith McWilliams
Elspeth Fielding had her own reasons for agreeing to live in a rustic cabin with James Murdoch. But after she met the reclusive novelist, the only important reason was him!

#442 HEAVEN SENT—Erica Spindler
A fulfilling career was Jessica Mann's idea of "having it all"—until she met Clay Jones and fulfillment took on a very different meaning.

#443 A FRIEND IN NEED—Cathie Linz
When Kyle O'Reilly—her unrequited college crush—returned unexpectedly, Victoria Winters panicked. She *refused* to succumb to her continuing attraction, but she could hardly kick him out—it was his apartment.

#444 REACH FOR THE MOON—Joyce Thies
The second of three *Tales of the Rising Moon*. Samantha Charles didn't accept charity, especially from the high and mighty Steven Armstrong, but a twist of fate had her accepting far more!

AVAILABLE NOW:

#433 WITH ALL MY HEART
Annette Broadrick

#434 HUSBAND FOR HIRE
Raye Morgan

#435 CROSSFIRE
Naomi Horton

#436 SAVANNAH LEE
Noreen Brownlie

#437 GOLDILOCKS AND THE BEHR
Lass Small

#438 USED-TO-BE LOVERS
Linda Lael Miller

Silhouette Intimate Moments

At Dodd Memorial Hospital, Love is the Best Medicine

When temperatures are rising and pulses are racing, Dodd Memorial Hospital is the place to be. Every doctor, nurse and patient is a heart specialist, and their favorite prescription is a little romance. This month, finish Lucy Hamilton's Dodd Memorial Hospital Trilogy with HEARTBEATS, IM #245.

Nurse Vanessa Rice thought police sergeant Clay Williams was the most annoying man she knew. Then he showed up at Dodd Memorial with a gunshot wound, and the least she could do was be friends with him—if he'd let her. But Clay was interested in something more, and Vanessa didn't want that kind of commitment. She had a career that was important to her, and there was no room in her life for any man. But Clay was determined to show her that they could have a future together—and that there are times when the patient knows best.
